SCENT OF PANIC

A CHRISTIAN ROMANTIC SUSPENSE

SULLIVAN K9 SEARCH AND RESCUE

LAURA SCOTT

Book 2

1

Wynona Blackhorse headed up to the front door of her neighbor's home. Her job working as an accountant for the tribal Council for the Shoshone Wind River Reservation didn't end until four thirty, and her four-and-a-half-year-old son, Eli, rode home from school with his 4-K kindergarten teacher, Shana Wildbloom, during the weekdays.

She knocked on the front door, then tried the door handle. Normally, Shana left it open for her, knowing she'd be there to pick up Eli.

The door was locked. She frowned, wondering what had caused Shana to do such a thing. A fission of concern snaked down her spine. She listened intently for a moment but heard nothing. She knocked again, harder.

No answer. The clouds overhead made the temperature feel cooler than usual, even though it was a balmy thirty-two degrees. She didn't see any lights on inside either. When there was still no response to her third pounding, she moved to the window to press her face against the glass.

She gasped when she saw Shana lying on the floor, blood staining her temple.

"Shana! Eli!" She slammed her hands against the glass so hard she was surprised it didn't break. Then she ran around to the next window, hoping to see Eli. But every room she could see into appeared empty.

Raw panic clawed up her throat, sending her pulse into triple digits. She ran all the way around to the back door, nearly sobbing in relief when she realized that one wasn't locked. Bolting inside, she knelt beside Shana.

"Shana! Wake up!" She shook the young woman's shoulder. "It's Wyn. What happened? Where's Eli?"

"Wyn?" Shana's eyelids fluttered open, and she stared up at her in confusion. "Who hit me?"

"I don't know. I just arrived here to pick up Eli. What happened? Where's my son?" Sliding her arm behind Shana's shoulders, she helped her sit up.

"I—don't know. The man wore a face mask." Shana put her hand to her temple, grimacing at the blood. "I was playing with Eli when he entered the house and struck me."

Wyn noticed the building blocks scattered across the floor and could imagine the young preschool teacher playing with Eli. She rose on shaky legs and began searching the home in earnest. Maybe Eli had been frightened by the intruder and had run away to hide. But even as she looked inside closets, under the beds, and behind doors, she knew the masked man had taken her son.

She quickly returned to the living room. "Did you see what kind of car he was driving?" Remaining calm wasn't easy, but she needed all the information from Shana that she could get. "Can you remember anything else about him?"

"He was tall and lean with dark-brown eyes." Shana

closed her eyes for a moment. "Maybe a white pickup truck? I noticed one parked a few houses down the road but didn't think anything of it as we passed by."

The description wasn't very helpful, but she didn't take her anger and frustration out on her friend. Instead, she pulled her phone from her pocket and scrolled to a number she hadn't called in over five years. She had to unblock the number first. Then she drew a steadying breath and made the call. Willing her panic at bay, she waited for him to answer.

"Wynona?" The shocked surprise in Chase Sullivan's tone sent a warring chill washing over her. He was the last man she should call.

He was also the only man who could find her son.

Their son.

"Chase, I need help. My son is missing, and I need your K9 search and rescue expertise to search for him."

"Your son?" Again, there was no mistaking the shocked surprise. "I—didn't realize you were married."

"I'm not. I don't have time to discuss the details now, but I need you. I need you to head to the rez and help me find Elijah." After a pause, she added, "Please. A masked man took him from his babysitter. I'm in desperate need of your help."

"I'll be there as quickly as I can. In the meantime, I need you to gather several of your son's recently worn clothing together for my K9, Rocky, to use as a scent source. Have you called the tribal police?"

"Not yet." Their tribal police department was small and covered the entire reservation. She wasn't at all confident in their ability to find Eli.

"Make the call," Chase advised. "I'll be there as soon as possible." His reassuring tone didn't make her feel any better. She had never been to his ranch but had heard about it. She knew the ranch was located a good two hours from her current location. "Where are you?"

"Riverton." She gave him the location, they didn't use typical addresses on the rez, and her throat thickened with fear and worry. "Please hurry."

"I'll do my best. Call me if anything changes."

"I will." She gripped the phone tightly, trying not to imagine her son being injured or dead, and added, "Thank you."

"See you soon." Chase ended the call.

She didn't wear the cross necklace Chase had given her over six years ago, but she lifted her eyes to the overcast sky, desperately seeking the Lord's support and guidance. She lowered the phone and turned to see Shana sitting in a chair at the kitchen table, holding her head in her hands.

"I don't understand. Who could have done this?" Shana's voice was barely a whisper. "I know there's plenty of crime on the rez, but usually not something like this."

"I'll get you some ice." Battling a wave of helplessness, Wyn crossed to the freezer. After making an ice pack for the preschool teacher, she turned back to survey the room. There was no sign of Eli's coat, hat, mittens, and boots. She wanted to be relieved that the kidnapper didn't mean her son harm if he'd taken time to dress him for the weather, but she wasn't.

She also noticed Eli's stuffed black horse was missing too.

After making the call to the tribal police, who promised to send an officer to Shana's home, she debated if it would help to contact her father, Ogima Blackhorse, one of the tribal leaders of the Shoshone Reservation. Then she quickly decided against it.

Her father wouldn't provide the emotional support she needed right now. Their relationship had been strained over the last year, despite his giving her a job working for the tribal council. He wanted her to move away from Riverton, claiming the city had more non-Native Americans than those born to the land. And he was right about that. But rather than move to a city within the rez, she had been thinking of a very different change. One that involved moving off the reservation completely to Cody, Cheyenne, or Laramie—for Eli's sake. Her son had needs that the schools on the rez couldn't meet. She knew he needed to be enrolled in the public schools of Wyoming. That would mean getting another job, but she wanted her son to have the best education possible.

But that was a topic for another day. Right now, she needed answers to who had taken Eli and why.

She hurried back outside to scan the neighborhood for a sign of the white pickup truck. She headed down the street in the direction Shana would have taken to come home from school, but she didn't see any vehicles parked there.

It wasn't smart to pin her hopes on a glimpse of a white pickup, but that's all she had to work from. Describing the assailant as a tall, lean man with dark-brown eyes fit almost half the men on the rez.

The panic at knowing her son was out there alone with strangers was crippling. She abruptly turned and headed on foot toward her home that was two doors down from Shana's. She snagged her phone charger in case the masked kidnapper called with some sort of ransom demand, then continued down the hall to her son's room. It didn't take long to place Eli's dirty clothes from yesterday into a bag. The fact that his shirt was stained from their spaghetti dinner made tears fill her eyes.

Would the kidnappers feed Eli? Would they keep him warm and sheltered from the wind, cold, and snow?

Her knees buckled, and she bowed her head and began to pray.

"Lord Jesus, I know You died to save me. Please spare my son's life. Please!" For a moment, she wondered if she was being punished for her sins. For the mistakes she'd made. For the secrets she'd kept.

A sob welled in her throat. Was this her fault? Was her little boy suffering at the hands of strangers because of her?

A Bible verse flashed through her mind. *In whom we have redemption through his blood, even the forgiveness of sins (Colossians 1:14).*

Swallowing hard, she lifted her head, willing the panic at bay. She'd learned about forgiveness of their sins. She needed to keep her faith in Jesus.

And in Chase's ability to find their son, before it was too late.

A DARK SENSE of dread rolled through Chase Sullivan's mind as he drove his specially designed K9 SUV down the highway toward Riverton. Six months ago, he'd taken a very similar path to the rez. He'd searched for a lost child, then, too. Nausea churned in his belly. What if he had the same outcome this time? Rocky had found the child, but too late. The little girl had been found dead at the bottom of a ravine.

Chase couldn't bear the thought of failing to rescue a second child.

He pushed his speed as much as he dared considering he was pulling a trailer. He'd decided to bring two snow machines. He knew the reservation had acres and acres of open land with very limited road access. In many cases, the direct line between two places couldn't be traveled by car, only by four-wheelers in the summer and snowmobiles in winter.

Using the rearview mirror, he glanced at his K9, Rocky. The large male Norwegian Elkhound was stretched out in the back crate area, looking around with interest. Rocky's fluffy fur belied his name but matched the dog's temperament to a T. Elkhounds could be incredibly stubborn and independent, and while Chase fought to be the alpha in their relationship, Rocky didn't always go along with the plan.

But Rocky was a good tracker and loved the snow as much if not more than Maya's husky, Zion. Rocky considered the search game a challenge, whereas Maya's Zion played to please her handler. They were both good at their jobs, while being different in temperament. And both dogs had high, ridiculously curled tails that often made him smile.

He wasn't smiling now. He hadn't seen Wynona in over five years, since the plane crash that had killed his parents. At the time, he'd had his own business as a hunting and fishing guide. He'd met Wynona in the town of Lander where she'd worked. They'd hit it off, and he had fallen hard for her. He'd hoped to marry her, but her father had not given his permission. Before Chase could find a way to win Wynona's father over, his parents had died.

He'd sold off his half of the Wyoming Wilderness Guide company to his partner David Cooksey to head home to the ranch. His oldest sister, Maya, had done the same thing, giving up her career in law enforcement and moving home from Cheyenne. It had never been an option not to head home to support their seven younger siblings. The property had once been an exclusive dude ranch, but it had been Maya's idea to change it into a search and rescue operation as a way to honor their dead parents. The siblings had spent weeks trekking through the wooded mountains in the approximate location that their parents' plane had gone down, without finding anything. No sign of the plane or their parents' bodies.

Only after the devastating loss did they discover the extent of their parents' wealth. He and Maya had been named the executors of the Sullivan trust and worked with the lawyers to make sure the ranch and all their siblings would be cared for into the future. Soon, all the siblings wanted to be a part of the search and rescue operation. The Sullivan K9 Search and Rescue Ranch was born and continued to flourish over the years as they successfully ran missions that had garnered them plenty of attention.

Yet it bothered Chase that they'd never found their parents. And while summers were typically their busiest season, he and his siblings often used whatever breaks they had in their schedules to continue their search efforts.

The trip down memory lane was his way of justifying why he'd left Wynona behind over five years ago. And he'd tried to reach out to her several times, without a response. He'd even gone back to the reservation to see her in person, but she'd moved, and he didn't know where she'd gone. He'd always intended to go back, to try again, but suddenly there were dozens of search and rescue operations that needed their expertise. The weeks had stretched into months, which had stretched into years.

Even six months ago, when he'd searched for the lost child, he'd thought he would run into her, but he hadn't.

And since the outcome had been grim, he and Rocky hadn't lingered.

Deep down, he'd known Wynona must have found someone else; otherwise, she would have returned one of his calls. Now that he knew about her son, he understood she'd moved on.

That she'd called him now was a testament to her level of desperation. He should have asked more questions about the child. Rocky was good, but he was worried about how they'd find a toddler in these wintery conditions. He called her back using his hands-free function.

"Chase? Where are you?" Wyn's voice was tense.

"I should be there in thirty minutes. I need you to fill me in on what happened so we can get to work as soon as I arrive."

"Eli was with Shana, his preschool teacher. I came to pick him up after work and found Shana lying on the floor bleeding from a wound on her temple. She said a masked man came into her house and assaulted her." Wyn's voice thickened. "I searched the house, but Eli is gone, along with his coat, hat, boots, mittens, and his stuffed horse."

"Did Shana recognize the man who came inside?"

"No. She described him as tall, lean, and with dark-brown eyes. His features were covered in a face mask." She paused, then added, "Shana noticed a white pickup truck parked along the side of the road when she drove home with Eli. There's no sign of it now, but I gave that information to the tribal police."

He hated to admit the situation sounded grim. "Okay. I'll be there soon. Send me a copy of the picture you provide the tribal police. Keep asking Shana questions. Witnesses often remember details later when the initial shock wears off." At least, that's what Maya had told him.

"I will. Please hurry." She ended the call before he could even answer.

By the time he pulled up in front of the home Wyn had described, his muscles were tense with fear and dread. His phone had pinged with the incoming text of the little boy's photo, but he hadn't dared take his eyes off the road to look at it. Darkness was falling, and the lack of street lighting on the reservation would make the upcoming search that much more difficult. Before he could slide out from behind the wheel, Wyn ran out to the car.

"Thanks for coming." Her dark eyes were wide with fear as she held up a plastic bag. "I have Eli's clothes."

"Okay." He released the back hatch, and Rocky immediately jumped down, then lowered his head and lifted his hindquarters to stretch his back. "Rocky, come."

The Elkhound eyed him for a moment, then trotted over with his head and tail up as if he were a king agreeing to meet with a peasant.

Chase put a hand on Wynona's arm. "Friend. This is a friend."

Rocky sniffed her feet, her hands and coat, then wagged his tail. The dog was friendly enough as long as he wasn't being ordered around.

"Good boy," Wynona whispered. Then she cleared her throat and looked up at him expectantly. "I spoke with the tribal police, and Shana gave her statement as well. Where will you and Rocky start?"

"Here, since this is the last place Eli was seen." He glanced down at his dog. "Give me a minute to prepare Rocky for work." He reached for the bag containing Eli's clothes, then headed toward the rear hatch. Thankfully, Rocky followed.

Chase quickly looped Rocky's vest over his torso and

cinched it tight. Rocky's nose lifted to the air, already anxious to explore. He clipped on a utility belt that contained various items that may come in handy during a search. He had a handgun but decided against pulling that out now.

When he was ready, he filled a small collapsible bowl with water and offered it to the K9. Moistening the dog's mucus membranes enhanced their scenting ability and was a routine part of their searches. Rocky ignored the water, looking away. This was one of their little tussles that made Chase grind his teeth in frustration.

Giving up on the water, he opened the bag and held it for Rocky. "This is Eli." He was relieved when Rocky buried his snout into the clothing. At least his stubborn K9 liked to work. "Eli," he repeated. Then he added excitement to his tone. "Are you ready? Are you ready to work? Search! Let's search for Eli!"

Rocky's tail wagged back and forth, and the dog didn't hesitate. Despite his dislike for being given orders, Rocky lifted his nose into the air and sniffed for several long seconds. Then he wheeled and trotted to the sidewalk leading up to the house.

Wynona ran forward to follow, but he grabbed her arm, holding her back.

"Don't interfere," he warned. "Stay back so Rocky has room to work."

Her expression hardened for a moment, but then she gave a jerky nod. "I understand."

He offered what he hoped was a reassuring smile. This situation was different from the search six months ago, and if she knew how that one had turned out, she didn't let on. "Don't worry, Rocky is very good at his job."

On cue, the Elkhound sat at the front door and gave a

sharp bark. That was Rocky's alert. He wasn't quiet about it the way Zion and some of the other dogs were.

"Good boy," he praised, but he didn't offer the red ball as a reward. "Search for Eli!"

Rocky whirled, sniffed along the sidewalk again, this time trotting to the road. When his K9 partner turned to keep going, he hastened to follow. Wynona's concern radiated off her, but she stayed where she was.

Chase was surprised when Rocky went a good sixty yards down the road before stopping to sniff a particular area with interest. He stayed back, waiting for Rocky's signal.

It came a second later. The dog sat and let out a sharp bark.

"Is that a real alert?" Wyn asked, her voice shaky. "Does your dog believe Eli was there?"

"Yes, that's exactly what Rocky is telling us." He pulled a flashlight from his belt and carefully approached the location, playing the light over the street. There wasn't any fresh snow covering the ground; the road must have been plowed or shoveled since the last snowfall. But he paused when he noticed several footprints in the snow along the side of the road.

He drew the red rubber ball from his pocket and tossed it for Rocky. The dog loved playing with the ball and took off running, his curvy tail wagging from side to side.

Lowering to a crouch, he examined the footprints. As a hunting and fishing guide, he was more familiar with small and large game animal tracks than with human footwear. There was a partial tread left in the snow that matched a popular brand of outdoor boots that probably 80 percent of all men wore here in Wyoming.

He didn't see a smaller footprint that may have belonged

to Eli. He slowly rose and glanced back over his shoulder. Wyn was closer now, as if she was unable to stay away.

"Maybe you should take a look." He gestured for her to come closer. "Do you see any footprints that may belong to your son?"

She rushed forward and bent to examine the ground illuminated by his flashlight. The excitement in her expression quickly faded. "No. I don't see anything other than adult-sized boot prints, and those are crisscrossed, making it impossible to judge the size of the shoe."

He nodded. "That's my impression too. I have to assume your son was carried here, maybe set down briefly before being placed in the car."

"The white pickup truck," she whispered. "I think the driver of the truck waited here for Shana and Eli to arrive. Once he was convinced they were settled in, he pulled on his face mask and headed inside to grab my son."

It was a logical theory to a point. "Okay, do you have any idea why someone would take your son?"

"No, I've been racking my brain ever since I found out he was missing." Her voice hitched. "He's just a little boy. I don't understand what's going on!"

He watched as Rocky ran around with the ball in his mouth, then turned to face her. "Come on, Wyn. The obvious answer is that this is a custody dispute. Don't you think it's possible the child's father has come back for him?"

"No! This isn't about Eli's father." Her voice was so vehement he was taken aback. "I don't know why Eli has been taken. I've been waiting for a call for some sort of ransom demand, but there's been nothing!"

He frowned. "How do you know for sure the boy's father isn't the one who took him? The fact that there hasn't been a ransom demand means this is personal. And I can't think of anything more personal than a father who might be making a desperate move to be a part of his son's life."

"You don't know what you're talking about." The words were bitter.

He sighed, striving for patience. "Okay, then help me understand. Because I'm getting the feeling that there's something you're not telling me."

She turned and stared off into the distance. Then she finally turned back to face him. "The reason I know this isn't a custody issue is because you are Eli's biological father."

The blood drained from his face. He was the boy's father? A wave of anger hit hard. He grabbed her shoulders, barely managing not to shake her senseless. "I'm his father? Why am I just hearing this now? Why didn't you tell me back when you discovered you were pregnant?"

Her eyes glittered with tears, but she didn't fight to pull out of his grip. She simply stared at him. "That's not important now. Eli is missing, and we need to work together to find him."

He tightened his grip, then abruptly released her. He grabbed his phone and opened the picture she'd sent earlier. A solemn-faced little boy stared back at him. He had his mother's dark hair and eyes, but Chase could see his chin in the boy's features.

He turned away, battling his anger. His son! He had a son! Yet he knew she was right. This wasn't the time to rehash the past. He could hate her for what she'd done, but that wasn't going to help.

The son he didn't know he had was missing. And other than a partial boot print and tire tracks that likely belonged to a white pickup truck, he had no idea how to find him.

2

———

Wynona had known the truth would come out the moment she'd contacted Chase. Had known there would be consequences, but they didn't matter as much as finding her son.

Finding Eli alive and well had to come first.

"What's next?" She pushed the question through her tight throat. "Where do we begin to search?"

Chase opened his mouth but seemed to think better of whatever he'd been about to say. "We need to canvass the neighbors, see if anyone noticed the white truck."

Her heart sank. The looming darkness only made her more keenly aware of the passing time. And Eli was afraid of the dark. Something she highly doubted the kidnapper would care about. "The tribal police officers already did that. They told me nobody saw anything suspicious."

Chase turned to scan the road. This section of town wasn't highly populated. People on the rez liked being far apart from their neighbors. And one thing the reservation had in abundance was land.

"We need to ask them again." He glanced at her. "Maybe coming from you as his mother will convince them to talk."

She frowned. "There's no reason the people living here would lie to the police. Not when it comes to a missing child."

He sighed. "Okay, the only other idea I have is driving around to look for a white pickup truck. Unless you can give me some idea as to who took him." His blue gaze sharpened. "A spurned boyfriend? Someone seeking revenge?"

She almost lashed out at him but managed to hold back. He had every right to ask these questions. This was his area of expertise after all. "My only relationship since we were together ended by mutual agreement. I can't imagine Dorian King assaulting Shana and taking Eli. He would have no reason to do such a thing."

"We still need to talk to him." He held her gaze. "What about Shana, the teacher? Is she seeing anyone?"

"Not that I'm aware of." She felt as if they were grasping at straws. The Wind River Reservation was huge, roughly two million acres with less than twenty thousand residents scattered across the land. Eli could be anywhere. She abruptly turned to head back toward Shana's. Concern for Eli had dulled her senses to the cold, but she realized she was beginning to shiver. "I'll ask her."

"Come, Rocky," Chase called. The dog didn't immediately come to Chase's side but ran in a circle first before trotting toward him. He held out his hand for the ball, but the K9 dropped it on the ground.

Chase let out a sigh as he bent to retrieve it. "I'm not in the mood, Rock. Don't push me."

If things were different, she may have been amused by the way Chase stared down his fluffy dog in a battle of wills.

But there was no room in her heart for joy. Not while Eli was missing.

She headed into Shana's home. Eli's teacher was stirring a pot of soup on the stove. Shana winced with guilt when she saw Wyn standing there. "I need to eat something to quell the nausea in my stomach."

"Probably from the head injury." She couldn't blame Shana for making dinner. The hour was going on seven o'clock, and normally, she'd be making dinner too. "I—we need to ask you some personal questions."

Behind her, Chase entered the home with his large dog. Shana's eyes widened at the sight of the animal, but she didn't protest. "Go ahead. Ask me anything."

"Have you been involved in a contentious breakup recently? Is there anyone in your past who could have decided to do this to get back at you?"

"That makes no sense. Eli isn't my son," Shana protested. But when Wyn continued to stare expectantly, she added, "I was seeing a man last year who I discovered had a secret drug problem. His name is Henry White, and I haven't seen him in months. I will say that if Henry had come here, he wouldn't take Eli. He'd have held me at knifepoint for money." Shana's expression turned grim. "He has stolen from me before, that's how I discovered he was using drugs. He wouldn't have the patience to hold a child for ransom. He's all about making a quick buck."

The ransom part was concerning. Why hadn't anyone reached out to her asking for money? If the man who'd taken Eli was indigenous to the rez, he would know her father was one of the tribal leaders and assume she had access to money.

She didn't consider Henry White as a viable lead, but

one glance at Chase convinced her he intended to check him out. Dorian too, she assumed, and she wanted to scream in frustration.

They were wasting precious time. Minutes that should have been spent scouring the area.

"Where does Henry live?" Chase asked. "We'll pay him a visit."

Shana sighed. "Last I knew, he lived in a trailer near the casino. He worked there for a while, until he showed up for work high on drugs. They fired him."

The casino was a good twenty-five miles away. She turned to look at Chase. "Dorian lives here in Riverton. We can try him first, then head out to Ethete. But I don't see why either of these men would take my son."

Chase had picked up one of the blocks from the floor, and she knew he was imagining their son playing with them. Resisting the urge to snatch it from his hands, she turned back to Shana.

"Will you please call me if you remember something?"

"Of course. I feel terrible this happened." The side of Shana's temple was red and swollen from the force of the blow. At least the cut had stopped bleeding. "I don't like knowing I failed your son."

"You didn't." She forced a brittle smile. "The man who took him is responsible. Not you. Just call me if you think of anything that may help."

"I will." Shana glanced pointedly at Chase and arched a brow. Shana probably figured out he was Eli's father, so she gave a slight nod, acknowledging her suspicions. Then she turned away.

"Wynona, could this be related to your job?" Shana asked.

She spun to face her. The thought hadn't occurred to her. "I'm not sure how taking Eli solves anything for the tribal elders."

"What's your job?" Chase asked.

She glanced at him. "I'm an accountant for the tribal council. I've recently started an audit, but I haven't found anything unusual. And as I said, I can't imagine why anyone would think that taking Eli would change that." She shrugged. "The truth is, if I quit my job today, they'll just hire someone else."

There was a long moment as Chase considered that. "Something to think about."

She resisted the urge to lash out at him. She wanted to be doing something. To be physically searching for Eli. "Let's go." She brushed past Chase to head outside. "We need to keep an eye out for the white pickup truck along the way."

Chase and Rocky followed close behind. Chase gestured toward his vehicle. "We'll take mine, as it's specifically designed to keep Rocky safe. And I need five minutes to feed him."

"Of course." She stopped abruptly, noticing the trailer for the first time. "What's in there?"

"Snow machines." He used his key fob to open the back hatch. Then he rummaged in the back before pouring kibble into a dish for his dog. He made Rocky sit and wait before giving him the signal to eat. It appeared that as far as food went, Rocky was willing to cooperate with Chase.

"Why?" She hadn't expected him to bring them. The stenciling announcing the Sullivan K9 ranch along the SUV was also something she hadn't anticipated.

"Hauling the trailer cost me some time in getting here,

but we have options if Rocky catches Eli's scent and leads us off-road." He shrugged. "Besides, some of the roads out here aren't great to start with. Many are barely dirt tracks that don't see a plow."

She hated to admit being impressed with his foresight. The fact that he'd considered all possibilities was heart-warming. He'd taken her request seriously, even before he'd known Eli was his son.

She reached for the front passenger door. "Good to know."

He took care of his dog, then slid in behind the wheel. As he pulled away from the side of the road, he asked, "Where does your former boyfriend live?"

"Turn right at the next intersection," she directed. "He lives between the community college and the cemetery."

"Okay," Chase said. She braced herself for additional questions, but he didn't voice them. Oh, he would, she knew, and likely sooner rather than later.

But for now, he appeared focused on the task at hand.

"Dorian works for the college. He's half Native American like me." She waved a hand. "I don't see why he would be involved in this."

"We need to check him off the list." His tone was even. "Once we know he's not involved, we can move on."

"You sound like a cop." She knew his older sister Maya worked as a police officer in Cheyenne. Or at least, she had until their parents were killed.

"I've learned a lot about running investigations from Maya." He darted a quick glance at her. "Many of our search and rescue operations involve a criminal component. We have to consider that's a possibility here too."

"I don't want to," she said in a hoarse whisper. "I know you're right that Eli may have been taken by some sort of child-trafficking organization, but I can't bear to think about it."

"I know. I can't stand the thought of that either." For a moment, a brief second in time, they were joined together by their shared panic, worry, and fear over Eli's fate.

Guilt hit hard. She knew she had wronged Chase, although he had done his part in this too. Still, she should have told him about his son.

She couldn't change the past. But she could impact their future.

She would ensure Eli had time to know his father once this nightmare was over. She would do anything once their son was back home where he belonged.

HARD. Soft. Hard. Soft. Eli rocked back and forth on the sofa, holding a wooden block in one hand and his stuffy in the other. He liked them both.

Hard and soft. Hard and soft.

"You hungry, kid?" The smelly man called him kid rather than his name. Eli. Eli Blackhorse.

Hard. Soft. Hard. Soft.

"He ain't too bright," the scary man mumbled. "Not sure why he's so important."

"Doesn't matter. We're being paid to keep an eye on him." The smelly man raised his voice louder. "I hope you like pizza, kid."

"I'll go pick it up." The scary man pulled on his coat but didn't use the face mask the way he had before. "At least we don't have to worry about him creating a ruckus."

Eli continued rocking back and forth. He was hungry. And he liked pizza, but only cheese pizza. Nothing else on it.

He was too scared to tell the two men that, though. Instead, he kept his head down and rocked.

Hard. Soft. He looked at his horse stuffy. Seeing it reminded him of his mom. She said the stuffy was from his grandfather because of their last name, Blackhorse.

Tears pricked his eyes, and his nose was running again. It had runned all during school too. He swiped at his nose with his sleeve. He didn't want to cry in front of the men. He was afraid to make them mad. They'd left him alone as long as he was quiet. And being quiet was his superpower.

That's what his mommy said.

Hard. Soft. Hard. Soft.

The scary man left the house, but he didn't watch him go. There was only one man there now, which he thought was a good thing. And Eli knew his mommy would be there soon.

She always came for him. No matter what.

It took every ounce of willpower not to lash out at Wynona for keeping his son a secret for over four years. Four years that he'd never get back.

And his despair over the possible outcome of this search haunted him. He couldn't, wouldn't fail this time.

Please, Lord Jesus, please protect Eli!

"Turn here," she said. "Dorian lives in the second house down from the apartment building."

He'd forgotten how dilapidated many of the homes were here on the rez. Shana's neighborhood had been one of the nicer ones. This area of town featured more trailer homes and prefab structures.

The one owned by this Dorian character appeared to be

the latter. He silently chastised himself for judging the guy based on the sole fact that he'd been the reason Wynona hadn't returned his calls.

"Looks like he's home," he said, breaking the tense silence. Lights glowed from inside the place. He didn't pull into the driveway because backing up the trailer was a pain. He put the gearshift in park, then turned in his seat to face her. "I'll bring Rocky with me. Rocky will let us know if Eli is or has been inside the place."

"Eli has been inside, so I'm not sure how that helps." She shrugged and pushed her door open. "But whatever you think is best."

He snagged her arm before she could get out. "How long ago?"

"Over a year." She glanced over her shoulder at him, clearly annoyed. "Why?"

He had no right to be angry, so he did his best to dial it back. "Okay, so if Eli has been here, then my plan of using Rocky won't work. Do you think Dorian will allow us to search the place?"

"I'm sure he will." She tugged out of his grip. "I told you our breakup was mutual."

He found that difficult to believe but didn't argue. As he'd told her earlier, the sooner they could scratch this guy off the list, the better. Chase opened the hatch for Rocky. The K9 jumped down and lifted his snout to the air. Then without waiting for his command, the dog bounded over to the sidewalk leading up to the house.

Chase hurried to catch up with him. The dog's independent streak could be annoying, but the Elkhound's hunting instincts were helpful when it came to the game of search. Rocky sniffed the ground but didn't alert. Dogs had over three hundred million olfactory receptors in their noses and could distinguish between various scents with surprising accuracy.

But scents that were outside didn't last long. The wind, rain, snow, and other elements eroded them away. Undaunted by Rocky's failure to alert outside the house, he waited for Wynona to catch up to them.

She rapped sharply at the door. Within seconds, he heard the muffled thumps indicating someone was coming. The door abruptly swung open revealing a man about five years younger than Chase with blond hair and dark eyes. The guy's eyes widened when he recognized Wynona.

"Dorian? Can we have a minute of your time?" she asked.

"Who's there?" a female voice asked. Before Dorian could protest, a slim, pretty Native American woman who looked to be barely of legal age came to join Dorian at the door. She wore a tight-fitting, long-sleeved shirt with a deep V revealing the upper edge of a bright-purple bra.

"Who are you?" the woman asked in a voice that did not sound happy. "We're busy."

"I've got this, Trina." Dorian's voice sounded impatient and faintly embarrassed. From the arched expression on Wynona's face, Chase assumed the young woman was one of Dorian's students.

No wonder Dorian hadn't resisted the breakup.

"We need to come inside," Chase said firmly. "Wynona's son is missing, and we need to make sure he's not here."

"Here?" Dorian looked shocked but readily opened the door. "Look, I don't think Eli could have made it all this way on his own. And I would have called if he'd shown up unexpectedly."

Chase realized Dorian was assuming the child had wandered away from home rather than being taken. Rocky brushed past him to enter the house, sniffing around the living room, then sitting near the sofa in front of the TV. The dog let out a sharp bark, startling both occupants of the home.

"Hey, I don't appreciate you bringing your dog in here," Dorian protested.

"He's working," Chase said. "Searching for Eli."

"Oh, well, okay." Dorian appeared chastised. "I guess I should have noticed his vest. But I'm telling you, I haven't seen Eli."

"Who are these people?" Trina asked irritably. "What right do they have to barge in here like this?"

"I'm looking for my son, and Dorian agreed we could look around to make sure he's not here." Wynona pinned the girl with a narrow look. "Unless you own the place, too, I'd recommend keeping quiet."

"Back off, Trina," Dorian said, looking nervous. Chase suspected the young woman was one of his students and her being there with him was breaking all kinds of rules. Not that he cared about that.

Chase stood by with Rocky as Wynona made quick work of searching the house, appearing devastated when there was no sign of their son. "Thanks, Dorian." She glanced pointedly at Trina, then added, "Don't worry. I have bigger things to worry about than whatever you're doing here."

Dorian flushed and began to object. Then he must have thought better of it. Chase turned to leave with Rocky. Wyn soon joined him.

"I told you that would be a waste of time." Her voice was low and harsh. "I don't want to drive all the way out to the casino. We need a different plan. There must be some way to find that white pickup truck."

He shared her frustration over their lack of a viable lead,

but he wasn't a miracle worker either. He strove to keep his tone nonconfrontational. "You live here, Wynona. I don't. I'm open to suggestions."

"I don't have one!" Desperation vibrated from her tone. She waved a hand at their surroundings. "If you took a child, where would you go? I can't think of a specific place the masked man could be hiding out. There are dozens upon dozens of abandoned homes. They could be anywhere."

"I understand. But getting upset and angry isn't going to help." He glanced at Rocky who was setting about to do his business. Something he should have anticipated after feeding him dinner. "Hang on, I need to clean up after my dog."

Wynona stood and stared up at the starless sky as he set about finding a bag to dispose of the waste. She looked so lost and forlorn; he ached to hold her. To comfort her.

He gave himself a mental shake. She'd lied to him, keeping his own son a secret. Yet he couldn't seem to stay angry with her.

At least not while Eli was missing.

The anger and hurt would hit him later, he knew. But for now, she was right in that they needed a better plan.

"I still think the drug addict could have something do to with Eli's disappearance." He fought to keep his tone calm. "The only other option is to simply drive around looking for the pickup truck. I'm willing to go that route, but I'm sure there's more than one around here."

"I know, it seems like a waste of time either way." She'd managed to get her emotions under control. "I'm sorry I snapped. I think we should stay in Riverton. I keep thinking they must be holding on to him for a reason." She pulled out her phone, staring down at the screen. "I almost wish the kidnapper would call with a ransom demand. At least we'd have something to work with."

He nodded, feeling the same way. "I have money to pay the ransom demand, if necessary."

She shrugged. "I can get money from my father too."

Over his dead body. But he didn't voice the thought. This not knowing was the worst. And really, the longer the kidnappers remained silent, the worse it was for Eli. He tried to take comfort in the fact that this situation was different from the one six months ago. Eli hadn't wandered out in the cold. Someone had taken him. Hopefully, they were keeping him warm and fed.

Maybe they shouldn't ignore the drug dealer. Desperate people did desperate things. After getting Rocky settled in the back seat, he slid in behind the wheel and waited for the heat to kick in. He turned toward Wyn. "Do you think the tribal police would check in on Henry White for us?"

Her expression brightened. "I can ask."

"Good, you do that." He shifted the car into gear and pulled away from the curb. If they were going to drive around looking for the white pickup truck, he should consider leaving the trailer of snowmobiles behind. He didn't like that idea, as they could be stolen. But pulling the trailer would also hinder his ability to chase the bad guys.

He listened as Wynona asked if the tribal officer could head out to visit Henry White, citing his drug habit and lack of employment as possible motives as to why he may have assaulted Shana and taken Eli. When she finished, she set the phone in her lap and sighed.

"He didn't sound enthused but agreed to head over to check on Henry." She shook her head. "I don't know what to do, Chase. Am I wrong not to drive to Ethete to speak with

Henry myself? What if Eli is there, and we could have already had him back by now?"

"Playing the what-if game isn't healthy," he said. "For one thing, if Henry wanted money, he'd have called you by now, right?"

"Yes. I'm sure he would have."

"Okay, then. Let the police do their part. If Eli is there, we'll know soon enough." He glanced at his fuel gauge. "I'm going to need to stop at the gas station."

"I understand." She was quiet for a moment, then said, "It seems wrong to eat while Eli is missing, but I'm hungry."

"I am too." He glanced at her. "It's not helpful to imagine the worst. No matter why this guy has taken Eli, we need to assume they'll feed him and keep him warm."

She shook her head. "You don't understand. Eli—" She stopped and frowned, then sat forward excitedly. "Chase, is that a white pickup truck?"

He saw the vehicle at the same moment she had. The white and more-rusty-than-not pickup truck was parked in front of a tavern called the Silver Spur. There wasn't enough room to park next to the truck while hauling his trailer, so he pulled into the side parking lot and found a spot in the back. He'd barely stopped the vehicle when she pushed out of the car.

"Wynona, wait!" He hit the button to open the hatch, then slid out of the car. "Rocky will tell us if Eli was in there!"

She ignored him, quickly crossing the parking lot. Thankfully, Rocky was still raring to go, so he turned his attention to his K9 partner.

"Are you ready? Search! Search for Eli!"

The dog eagerly lifted his snout to the air, sniffing with interest. Chase wanted to follow Wynona to make sure she didn't get herself into trouble, but he didn't leave his dog. He was confident that Rocky would be the key to locating Eli.

And he really, really hoped that nobody was stupid enough to head inside a bar while leaving a four-year-old out in the car alone in temperatures that were dropping like a rock.

The dog made a back-and-forth pattern of sniffing the area, similar to the way many of his siblings' K9s did. Chase stayed back, knowing better than to try to lead the dog to the area where he wanted him to work. Granted, the rationale for that approach was to prevent a K9 from providing a false alert simply to please their handler.

Not something Rocky would do. Chase knew his high-energy K9 played the search game because he liked it. Because he wanted to succeed, and because Rock enjoyed the hunt. Not because Chase asked him to.

After what seemed like forever, but was only a few minutes, Rocky made his way toward the front of the Silver Spur. Chase lengthened his stride to keep up. The dog was good about not getting too distracted by other interesting scents, but once in a while, something really intrigued him.

Thankfully, his dog appeared to be focused on Eli, which was a good thing.

Wynona came toward him, her expression grim. "I didn't see anything in the truck that would indicate Eli was inside."

He gestured toward Rocky. "He hasn't alerted yet either. And he would if he caught Eli's scent."

While Rocky continued searching the area, he strode toward the truck. It looked in even worse shape up close, and he suspected that Shana would have noticed if the truck along the side of the road was this battered. The inside of the vehicle was a disaster, dozens of fast-food wrappers and empty oil bottles along with at least twenty beer cans.

Wynona was right. Nothing to indicate a child had been inside. He silently prayed the kidnappers wouldn't be drinking and driving with Eli in the car.

Trying not to be dejected, he turned away. One truck down and far too many more to investigate.

At this rate, they'd still be searching by morning.

3

Wynona had never felt so helpless in her entire life. Not even when she'd realized she was pregnant with Chase's child and facing her father's sharp disappointment. Not that her father had stayed angry for long. Ogima was mush when it came to his grandson.

Where was Eli? Who had taken him? Why hadn't they called her?

If Chase was as disappointed as she was, he didn't let on.

"Come, Rocky." The dog ignored him at first, but then wheeled and ran halfway down the parking lot before returning to his side. "Always on your own timeline," Chase muttered as he bent to stroke the dog's fur. "You never give up trying to maintain the upper hand."

For the second time, she found their interaction amusing. But she couldn't manage a smile. Seeing Chase after so long only reminded her of how much she'd cared about him. But that was before.

Too much had happened to pick up where they'd left off. And for all she knew, Chase was involved with someone else by now. Although the way he'd stared daggers at Dorian had reeked of jealousy. Ridiculous, as Trina's presence had explained why they'd broken up. Commitment to a relationship was not Dorian's strong suit.

"We'll stop at that gas station up the street." He opened the back hatch and gestured for Rocky to get inside.

"Looks like they have food." She joined him up front. The heat blasting from the vents was a welcome relief. She'd grabbed warmer clothing when she'd stopped at her house for Eli's things, but the wind still stole her breath. There were rolling hills and scattered woods to the north of Riverton where herds of wild buffalo and wild horses along with other large game like moose and elk grazed throughout the year. The city teemed with visitors during the summer months, especially those who wanted to see what it was like on an Indian reservation. Winters could be far more desolate. She shivered and snuggled down in her thick coat. "I'm not picky. Anything quick and easy works for me."

"Okay." He pulled away from the side of the road and continued down to the gas station. He pulled up to the pump closest to the building. She glanced over her shoulder to notice the trailer barely cleared the road.

It must be difficult to maneuver the long trailer and extra weight behind them. Would they even need the snow machines? She hoped not.

"Go inside and get warm," he said. "I'll be in as soon as I finish filling the tank."

She nodded and hurried inside. The scent of tobacco and stale coffee made her stomach churn. Maybe she wasn't as hungry as she'd thought. When she spotted several slices of pizza in a warmer, she headed toward it. Seeing the cheese pizza gave her pause, and her throat grew thick with emotion. Cheese pizza was one of Eli's favorite meals.

Would he eat whatever the kidnapper gave him? She doubted it.

She must have stayed there staring at the food longer than she realized because Chase came up behind her. "Starving yourself won't make Eli feel any better."

"I know." Logically, he was right. She needed strength to find her son. She gestured to the pizza slices. "Eli loves cheese pizza."

"I wouldn't know," Chase said, an edge to his tone. But then she heard him sigh. "Sorry, do you want me to get one for you?"

"Yes, please." She didn't have a lot of cash on her. "I can use my debit card."

"I'll take care of it." He nodded toward the restrooms. "I need a minute, then I'll get the food."

She followed him to the restrooms, realizing he was right to use the facilities while they were there. She needed to do a better job of planning ahead. If Eli were here . . .

She stopped herself from continuing that thought. As Chase said, there was no point playing the what-if game. The only way to get through this was to think positive. To believe they would find their son. And to believe Eli wouldn't be hurt.

When she emerged from the bathroom, she found Chase was already at the counter buying their food along with bottles of water and a box of granola bars. As he handed cash to the clerk, she belatedly realized she never offered to pay for his services.

"I, um, didn't ask how much you charge for this sort of thing," she said as they headed back outside to the SUV. In the distance, a pair of red taillights disappeared into the night. Not unusual to see traffic on the roads. Now that darkness had fallen, their ability to even see a white pickup truck was diminished. They'd have to be right on top of the vehicle to identify the make, model, and color. She slid into the passenger seat, waiting as he got behind the wheel. "Rumor has it that you and your family only accept dog food as payment for services."

"That's true, but I would search for any child for free regardless." His jaw tightened. "If I had known Eli was my son, I'd have brought several of my family members with me. I'm not sure that it will do much good to have them swarm the area now, though. But if we learn anything about where Eli may be, I'll call them to help find our son."

She winced, accepting the pizza from him. It had not occurred to her to have him ask for his family to accompany him. Would it help to have more eyes on the road looking for the white truck? Maybe. Although it could also be a colossal waste of time. "I understand. Thank you."

He started the car but didn't pull away. Instead, he closed his eyes for a minute. By the time she realized he was praying, he was finished. He took a large bite of his pizza, shifted into gear, and pulled out onto the main road leading through town.

She silently thanked God for the food and added another prayer for Eli's safety before trying her meal. The pizza tasted like cardboard, but that didn't matter.

The food was nothing more than fuel. Something to keep her going until she had her son back in her arms. "Where are we going?"

Chase shrugged. "We'll go up and down some of these streets. There aren't a lot of garages here, so maybe we'll find more white pickup trucks to test with Rocky's nose."

She nodded. It wasn't as if she had a better plan.

"Tell me about that job of yours," he said after a few

minutes. "I didn't know you had left Lander to return to the rez."

"You probably remember my father is one of the tribal leaders. He asked me to help with bookkeeping for the council." She frowned as the timing suddenly seemed suspicious. "I did tell them last week that I had begun an audit. I noticed one hadn't been done for at least five years, and they should be done annually or at the very least biannually."

"I can't help but wonder if your job is a part of this," Chase said. "I mean, if the goal of taking Eli isn't ransom, then why would they bother?"

"I have no idea." She wasn't sure what to think. "But as I said, if I'm out of the picture, someone else would step in and take over. And if they wanted to stop me from doing the audit, why go after Eli? Why not attack me directly?"

"Good point," Chase admitted. "I guess it could be that the kidnapper is waiting until morning since there's no way to access money at this hour of the night."

She felt sick at the thought of the kidnappers making a ransom demand come morning. It wasn't like she had a lot of money in her bank account. She'd hand every last dollar over to them if it meant freeing her son, but she doubted that would be enough.

What if they asked for some astronomical amount of money? Chase had offered to pay, but she wasn't sure he had enough funds either.

The pizza she'd eaten churned in her gut. Would the masked intruder go as far as to hurt her son if they couldn't pay?

She closed her eyes, then forced them open. No, she needed to stay focused. She turned and scanned the street outside her passenger door window. She needed to keep on high alert for a white pickup truck. That was the only lead they had.

She couldn't bear the thought of missing it.

"Hurry up, we gotta get the kid out of here!"

Eli was startled by the scary man's harsh words. He tightened his grip on the block and his stuffy.

Hard. Soft.

"Why?" Smelly Man complained.

"There was a search and rescue rig at the gas station." Scary Man sounded upset. "I'm sure they're looking for the kid!"

"How could they know we have him here?" Smelly Man asked. "We made sure nobody saw us."

"I didn't say they know our exact location, stupid." Scary Man punched Smelly Man in the arm, making Eli flinch. Would he get punched too? He went back to his rocking. "I'm saying they're too close for comfort. We need to implement plan B."

"That's going to cost more money," Smelly Man argued. "I don't wanna ask the boss for more, do you?"

"Shut up and grab the kid!" Scary Man shouted so loudly tears leaked down Eli's face. He gripped the toys harder now, so hard his hands hurt. "The money doesn't matter if we're found. We have a secondary location to use in the case of an emergency. This counts in my book. We need to get out of here. And we'll take both vehicles, understand? You take the kid in your truck. Follow me to the next house."

"Okay, okay. Hold your horses." Smelly Man rose from

the kitchen chair, staggering a little. Eli kept his head down but knew the smelly man was coming toward him. "Come on, kid. You heard him. We gotta go."

Eli slid off the couch. He stood quietly as the smelly man shoved his clenched hands into his coat sleeves. He managed to keep a hold of his toys, but the smelly man wrenched them from his hands and stuffed them into his pockets.

"You're a weird kid," he muttered as he zipped the coat shut. Then he crammed a hat on Eli's head and forced mittens over his hands. Eli didn't like wearing mittens. He wanted to pull them off so he could hold the toys in his pockets.

He wanted to feel them in his hands. Hard. Soft. Hard. Soft.

But it was cold outside. His nose ran again, and he swiped at it with the sleeve of his coat. When the smelly man set him in the back of the truck, he didn't protest. At least Scary Man was going in the other car.

Eli rocked back and forth in the back seat, hoping his mommy would get there soon. He was tired and hungry and wanted to go home.

CHASE FINISHED HIS PIZZA, doing everything in his power not to lash out at Wyn. He was angry with her for keeping Eli a secret, yet he was also just as angry with her father.

He had not expected the guy to refuse his request to marry Wynona. And when he asked why, the old man had simply said he wasn't good enough for Wyn, and he wasn't Native American.

As if it was her father's decision that his daughter would only marry someone from the tribe. Chase had never heard anything so ridiculous. And since he could be as stubborn as his K9, Rocky, he'd let the old man know the decision should be Wynona's not his.

Looking back, he shouldn't have asked permission in the first place. Maybe if he'd had proposed to Wynona, she'd have accepted, and they'd have been married and living together on the ranch when she'd discovered she was pregnant.

And they'd be raising their son, together. As a family.

The image of Eli's somber face was burned in his memory. He wasn't sure he could forgive her for not telling him the truth. Especially since he should have been there for her. It burned to know that if things were different, Eli's last name would be Sullivan, not Blackhorse.

Well, his son wouldn't be a Blackhorse for long. He wasn't sure how he'd convince Wynona to allow him to change Eli's name, but his son would become a Sullivan as soon as humanly possible. The way it should have been all along.

And Wynona needed to know he wasn't about to let his son go without a fight.

Granted, they had to find him first.

It was difficult not to imagine this search ending like his last missing child case. With the child's death.

He prayed like he'd never prayed before. After several long moments, he pulled himself together. He needed to stay positive.

"Maybe we should head back to your place." He glanced at her. "It might be smart to leave the trailer in your driveway."

She sipped her water. "I hate to backtrack. The one place we know for sure the kidnapper won't go is my place. I live two houses down from Shana. They'd want to avoid the scene of the crime."

"Wait, you live that close to her?" He frowned. "Is it possible the kidnapper thought Shana was you?"

"I can't see how. For one thing, she's a good eight years younger than I am." She waved a hand. "For people who live on the reservation, one Indian doesn't look exactly like the other."

He winced. "That wasn't what I meant. It's just that you both have long, dark, straight hair. You're both pretty, and Shana was sitting on the floor playing with Eli. I saw the blocks scattered about. Maybe the kidnapper saw them through the window and assumed you were there."

"Okay, so even if that is the case, what does it matter?" Wyn sounded exasperated. "Shana was hit, not killed. The goal was still to take Eli, regardless of who was watching over him."

"I don't know, I just keep thinking that maybe your job is related to all of this." He shared her frustration. Maybe he was on the wrong track. Without a ransom demand, there must be something else at play.

The simple truth was that he didn't want to consider the possibility that their son was in the hands of a child-trafficking ring. Maya had told him about how she'd found a young teenage girl who'd run away from home and had ended up in a prostitution ring. There was so much evil in the world that he knew little kids could be targeted for a similar reason.

The way he and Rocky had found Alecia dead six months ago had bothered Chase for months afterward, until

Maya had drawn him aside and reminded him that they were doing their best with the gifts God had bestowed on them. It would be highly unlikely that they'd find every single missing person they searched for.

Their parents missing for five years now was a primary example.

He'd done his best to move on. And he and his siblings turned to their faith rather than taking the situation personally when they failed to find their victim alive.

But failure was not an option tonight.

"Look, if you want to drop off the trailer, that's fine." Wyn's comment interrupted his thoughts. "You're the one who brought the snow machines along in case we needed to take a direct route between cities."

"I know." In truth, he was torn. He'd brought them because last month he and his brothers had used snowmobiles to get through a blizzard to find Maya and her now fiancé, Doug Bridges. Without the machines, they'd never have made it.

Winter weather could turn bad on a dime. And out here on the rez where there were more open areas without houses, the blowing snow was known to be wicked. Maybe he was better off keeping the trailer close.

"We can't drive around all night," he finally said. "I don't want to give up searching for Eli, but you know as well as I do he could be anywhere."

"Let's give ourselves another hour before we head back." She sighed. "I guess we should try to get some rest, even though I can't imagine I'll be able to fall asleep."

He reached out to touch her arm. "I know. But my vision is getting a little blurry. By daylight, we should be able to see white pickup trucks more clearly." He hesitated, then added, "It's likely the kidnappers are tucked in with Eli for the night. If they have the car hidden in a shed or garage, we'll never find it."

"Okay. One more hour." She turned to stare out her window. "I can't explain it, but I feel like Eli is being held somewhere nearby."

Likely wishful thinking on her part, but he couldn't blame her. If Eli had been taken to a different city on the rez, they'd never find him.

And somehow, he didn't think the tribal police would either. They weren't bad cops, but their resources were limited.

It made him mad that Wynona had chosen to raise their son here.

"Why didn't you call me?" The question came out sharper than he had intended. "I had a right to know about Eli."

She glanced at him, then turned to stare back out the window. "I was scared," she finally said.

"Of me?" That was the most ridiculous thing he'd ever heard. "I've never harmed a woman in my life!"

"Of you taking Eli away from me." She shook her head, still not looking at him. "I don't want to get into this now, Chase. I'm sorry, okay?"

"Not okay," he shot back. "You had no right to keep my son away from me."

"You left me, remember?" She finally turned to look at him. "You left me. For months, Chase. Then I needed to care for my father's sister who fell ill with cancer." Then she abruptly held up a hand. "Let's not do this. Eli is missing. I need to search for white pickup trucks. And so do you," she added. "We can hash this out later once Eli is safe."

He bit his tongue but grudgingly nodded. It wouldn't make things any easier in the long run if he continued taking his anger and frustration over the lack of progress on the case out on her.

But it wasn't easy to sit there knowing she'd lied to him by omission either.

He told himself the future was more important than the past. That while his son didn't know him now, that would change the minute they found him. He would be a part of his son's life moving forward.

There was no doubt in his mind that Eli would love living on the ranch. Interacting with their nine dogs, their four horses, and experiencing nature at its finest. Anna, their housekeeper, would cook him his favorite foods, and as the only Sullivan nephew, Chase knew the child would be spoiled by every one of his eight aunts and uncles.

Wynona could stay on the ranch, too, if she wanted to. But that would be up to her. She could control her fate. He'd already decided there was no way he'd allow his son to grow up on the rez.

Holding on to that silent promise was the only way he could bring himself to drop the subject of why Wynona had learned to hate and resent him to the point she had done this.

And while he drove, he couldn't bear to think of the possibility of failing in their mission to find Eli.

He took side streets, not that there were many available, to head back to the east end of Riverton and her home near Shana's. They had heard nothing from the tribal police on Shana's former boyfriend, which only reinforced his low opinion of their ability to find Eli.

"Is it always this dead around town at this hour?" Chase glanced at Wynona. "I realize it's ten thirty at night, but I expected there to be more activity." To his mind, it was strange that he didn't see many vehicles out on the road.

And other than the one truck in front of the Silver Spur, there wasn't a white pickup truck to be seen.

"In February?" She shook her head. "Too cold for people to be out and about. Besides, all there is to do is to drink at the bar. Those inclined to do that find it cheaper to drink at home. Poverty is still a significant issue here, despite the casino money coming in."

He grimaced. He'd nearly forgotten that when he'd been running his hunting guide business, February and March were their worst months revenuewise. He shouldn't be surprised that things were slower all over the state. Even here.

"It's not like those in small rural towns are living high on the hog," he said. "Other than the rich tourists that flock to the ski slopes in Jackson this time of year, winters are slow for most folks. I just thought there would be more activity here in Riverton."

"Poverty extends across the reservation." Her tone was testy. "The people here need jobs more than anything. And of course, less access to drugs."

Before he could ask more, a sharp crack of gunfire rang out. The steering wheel bucked beneath his hands as he fought to keep it on the road.

Chase instinctively punched the gas, desperate to put distance between him and whoever had fired at them. The SUV engine roared as it struggled to respond to the change while pulling the trailer.

"Are we hit?" Wyn asked.

"I don't think so." He couldn't be sure, but he thought it was possible the bullet had pinged off the hard covering over the sleds on the trailer. He mentally braced himself for more gunfire, but several for long minutes, there was nothing but silence.

He realized they were only two streets from Shana's house, which meant they were also close to Wynona's place.

Were they wrong about the kidnapper's intent? Maybe the real goal here was to eliminate Wynona.

Permanently.

4

Had the kidnapper taken shots at them? Wynona gripped the handrest tightly and peered into the darkness. She couldn't see anything suspicious but knew someone was out there.

The shooting attempt made no sense. Unless she and Chase had gotten too close?

She turned and grabbed his arm. "Maybe the kidnappers are trying to scare us off because they're hiding Eli nearby."

"I doubt they'd hold him this close to the original scene of the kidnapping." He glanced at her before turning onto the street where she lived. "But I'm going to take Rocky and search the area for the shooter. I don't like putting my K9 in danger, but we need to understand what's going on."

She swallowed hard. If the gunman hurt Chase or Rocky, she would feel responsible. And selfishly, she knew Rocky was their best chance at finding Eli. The way he'd alerted where the white pickup truck had been located and again at Dorian's house proved that the dog would be able to find her son if they were able to get close enough to the place he was being held. "Maybe we shouldn't do that."

"It's a risk I need to take." Chase looked grim as he parked along the side of the road in front of her house. "I doubt the shooter would be stupid enough to stick around. But he may have left evidence behind."

That possibility helped sway her opinion. "Okay, then I'm coming with you." When he frowned as if to argue, she tightened her grip on his arm. "Please, Chase. I can't just sit here worrying about you. And if we can find the gunman or his location where he was when he took that shot at us, he could lead us to Eli."

"Fine, but you'll need to stick close." He threw his door open and released the rear hatch. She released him to slide out of the car. Rocky appeared eager to go as he sniffed the area with interest. "Rocky, come."

This time, the dog obeyed Chase's command, trotting over to his side. Chase bent and ruffled his fur with his gloved hands. She stayed back, watching with interest. She'd heard rumblings about the Sullivan K9 search and rescue siblings, but seeing them in action was more impressive than she'd expected.

She tried not to stare at Chase as he worked with his K9. He'd only grown more handsome over the years.

"Are you ready to search?" Chase revved up the excitement in his tone. "Are you, boy? Search! Search for gold!"

Gold? She wanted to ask what that meant, but Rocky wheeled away from Chase and lifted his nose to the air. The dog moved in a circle, then abruptly bounded between her home and the one between her and Shana in the direction they'd come from.

Chase took off after him, so she broke into a run too.

This was what he'd meant by keeping up. Jogging with a bulky coat, hat, gloves, and snow boots wasn't easy, but if Chase could do it, so could she.

Rocky slowed his pace, his nose working constantly. She took a moment to catch her breath, hoping and praying the dog would find something.

And that the gunman wasn't sitting in a hiding spot, waiting for them to get close enough to shoot at them again.

The dog abruptly headed to the right, then bounded forward through an open area between homes. Rocky was light enough weightwise that he was able to walk over the top of the snow without breaking through.

She and Chase were not. Glancing back over her shoulder, she grimaced at the fact that they were leaving a blatant trail in their wake.

Then she took heart in knowing the shooter would have left his tracks behind as well.

Chase turned to follow Rocky. She slipped in the snow, but then regained her momentum. She managed to catch up to Chase just as she heard Rocky let out a sharp bark.

"What did he find?" She squinted, trying to see where Rocky was sitting.

"Not sure," Chase said in a low voice. "Stay behind me, okay?"

She understood he was trying to protect her. Shifting to the side, she did as he asked. It wasn't easy, as she couldn't see beyond his broad shoulders.

Then she caught a glimpse of pale skin and realized he had removed his right glove to hold a weapon. Swallowing a protest, she gripped the back of his coat and followed him around the corner of a dilapidated building. Not a house, but a shed of some sort.

She still couldn't see Rocky and began to worry the gunman was hiding nearby looking for the opportunity to spring out at them. But then Chase moved forward, and she caught a glimpse of tracks in the snow.

Human tracks and the faint impression of Rocky's paw prints.

The tracks led to a trailer home, but Rocky wasn't near the door the way she'd expected. The dog sat toward the end of a driveway marked with fresh tire tracks, and the Elkhound stared toward Chase expectantly.

"What did you find, Rock?" Chase asked, scanning the area as he approached the dog. She wanted to rush inside the trailer house but managed to hold back. Not only was the place dark inside, the recent tire tracks and lack of a white truck, or any other vehicle for that matter, indicated nobody was home.

But she wanted, needed to know if Eli had been there recently.

"Good boy," Chase proclaimed. "Good find, Rocky!" He slipped the gun back into his pocket and retrieved the red ball. He tossed it for the dog, then dropped to his haunches to peer down at the ground.

"I don't understand," she said, trying to see beyond his shoulder at what had caught his attention. "What is gold?"

"Gun powder and gun oil associated with weapons. And by association, bullets and shell casings." He put his glove back on to pick up the shell casing that had fallen into the snow, holding it up for her to see. "Maya has been working on cross-training our dogs to find guns. And Rocky did his part with this."

"Wow, that's amazing." She shot another worried glance around the area. This particular trailer house was at the end of a road that was probably a mile or so from her place. In following Rocky's path, they had gone farther than she'd realized. "Does that mean the shooter was standing here when he fired at us?"

Chase rose. "Actually, based on the trajectory of the shot and the location of the shell casing, I think the guy must have fired at us from inside his car."

She frowned. "And what, just happened to see us driving by?"

He shrugged, watching as Rocky ran in a circle with his ball. "It's not like the SUV and trailer are easy to hide. And that's my fault because I thought it would be a good idea to have our name and logo stenciled on the sides of the SUVs." He grimaced. "Maya might be right in that we should get the entire fleet repainted."

She could see his point. "I would like to think most people would support you and your family since you're providing a service to the community."

"That's what I had hoped too. But tonight's gunfire proves otherwise." He raised his voice. "Come, Rocky!"

The dog ignored him. Chase sighed.

She gestured to the tire tracks. "Is there a way to identify if these specific tire marks belong to a pickup truck?"

Chase turned away from Rocky to examine the tracks more closely. "I doubt it. Looks to me as if there was more than one vehicle that came down the driveway. See how they crisscross each other?" He walked out into the street. "Even out here there are two sets of tracks."

Rocky bounded over, his high curved tail wagging back and forth as he dropped the ball on the ground at Chase's feet. Chase grunted with annoyance as he bent to pick it up.

She had to admit that it seemed as if the dog purposefully waited to obey Chase's commands. She turned her attention back to the shell casing. "Are you going to call the tribal police to give them the casing?"

"Not yet." Chase gestured to the trailer. "Give me a minute to see if anyone is inside. If not, I'll ask Rocky to search for Eli's scent."

Her pulse spiked. "You really think Eli was here?"

"Not sure. But it occurs to me that the gunman may have been trying to scare us off." Chase leveled her a stern look. "Stay here with Rocky. This won't take long."

She nodded reluctantly. "Hurry."

Chase pointed at Rocky. "Stay!" Then he headed up to the trailer home. From her position next to Rocky, who surprisingly obeyed Chase this time, she held her breath as he moved from one window to the next. He paused briefly to try the front door, then moved on.

After a few minutes, he disappeared around the corner to check the rest of the home.

She forced herself to breathe, aware of the cold chill in the air now that she wasn't running through the neighborhood.

"So, Rocky, how do you like living on the Sullivan ranch?" She felt foolish for talking to the dog, but the way the Elkhound cocked his head and looked up at her made her think he was listening.

Just when she was about to go after Chase, he rounded the dwelling from the opposite side. To his credit, he had worked quickly.

"No sign of anyone inside." He quickly strode toward her. "And good news, the door is unlocked. It appears to me as if they left in a hurry. There are a couple of half-full beer bottles on the kitchen table." He reached down to put his hand on Rocky's head. The dog looked up at him. "Are you ready to work? Are you? Search! Search Eli!"

"Don't you need the scent bag?" she asked.

"Unfortunately, it's in the SUV." He shrugged. "Rocky is smart. I think he'll remember Eli's scent."

As if to prove him right, the dog began his zigzag pattern of sniffing along the ground. It didn't take long for the dog to end up at the front door of the trailer. He sat and let out a sharp bark.

"Good boy," Chase said, quickly heading to the door. He didn't take the ball from his pocket, though. Instead, he opened the front door and stepped inside. After a moment, a light flashed on. "Search! Search for Eli!"

With her heart lodged in her throat, Wyn came inside to watch Rocky work. And when the dog alerted right next to the sofa, it was all she could do not to cry.

Eli had been taken away. And as much as she was relieved to know Eli had been there, she and Chase were no closer to finding their son.

Or the men who had him.

STUNNED to realize the son he had never met had been held there inside the trailer, it took him a moment to reward his K9 partner for a job well done. "Good boy! Good find, Rocky." He reached for Rocky's ball, then hesitated.

This was technically a crime scene.

DNA from the beer bottles could be tested. A process that would take at least several days, even if he could convince the cops to put a rush on the results.

His soon-to-be brother-in-law Doug Bridges worked for the State of Wyoming Criminal Investigations Division. The state was too small for the local police departments to handle significant crimes, and the feds generally only got involved when criminals crossed state lines. Or for crimes occurring within national parks.

And larger crimes occurring on the Wind River Reservation. Like kidnapping?

Maybe.

"Okay, we need to get out of here." He winced as Wyn looked as if she might burst into tears at any moment. "The trailer needs to be processed for evidence."

"How soon can that be done?" She turned and headed back outside.

"I'll make some calls." He didn't want her to be depressed to know what the likely turn around is for the techs to even get there, much less process the evidence.

When they'd cleared the trailer, he pulled the ball from his pocket and tossed it for Rocky. The dog acted as if he'd been separated from his toy for hours instead of minutes, taking off after it, then running in circles.

The five-year-old Elkhound was a puppy at heart.

"Where do you think they took Eli?" Wyn asked. Then her eyes widened. "I know, I can access the tribal housing database to find out who owns this house and see if that same person owns any others."

"That's a good idea." He gestured toward the road. "We need to get back to your place."

She shivered and nodded. "The sooner the better."

"Rocky, come!" He didn't wait for the dog, knowing he'd respond in his own sweet time, but began retracing their steps. Five minutes later, Rocky bounded beside them still holding the ball in his mouth. Chase looked at the dog. "Hand."

The dog clearly didn't want to give up his toy, but after a

long moment, he dropped it on the ground. Chase scooped it up and put the ball in his pocket. Rocky tested his patience more often than not, but the K9 had performed exceptionally well for them tonight. Despite his stubborn independent streak, Rocky had given them what they'd needed.

He'd take the win. Especially knowing Eli had been alive and well when he was there, what, an hour ago? Maybe less?

Following their tracks back to the site of the shooting was easy enough, and it didn't take long to spot the SUV and trailer. He took a moment to examine the outside of the SUV and snowmobile trailer, finding the deep groove along the top of the trailer that had been made by the path of the bullet.

At least the sleds and the SUV weren't damaged, but he was still upset at how close the shooter had come to derailing their search.

Although if that had been the goal, the kidnappers had made the first of what he hoped were many mistakes. The shooter had underestimated their determination to find their son. Quite the opposite. The shooter had inadvertently led them straight to the location where they'd been holding Eli.

He and Wynona were one step closer to finding Eli. If the tribal housing authority records led them to a secondary location.

And if not? He winced, deciding not to head down that path. They needed to think positive. To stay focused.

To have faith in God. Something he'd struggled with over the years since losing his parents.

He quickened his pace, anxious to get inside so Wynona could start her search.

"Let me go inside first," he said, when they'd reached her

home. It was small but nicer than the trailer. He pulled out his gun. "I'll let you know when I've cleared the place."

She frowned but gave a jerky nod and pulled out her keys. "Here. I locked it when I left earlier this morning."

He unlocked the door and stepped inside. Being greeted by the familiar cinnamon and apple scent threatened to send him back in time to the early days of his relationship with Wynona.

The house was generally neat and tidy, although there were signs that a small child lived there. A booster seat on one of the kitchen chairs. A pair of small boots near the front door. It wasn't easy to stay focused on the task at hand.

After verifying the house was empty, he went back to the front door. "It's clear. Rocky, come."

The dog paused to lift his leg to pee on a snowbank, then trotted toward him. Chase stepped back so the dog could come in. The K9 lifted his nose to the air, sat, and let out a sharp bark.

"I'm surprised he's alerting on Eli's scent even though you didn't ask him to search," Wyn said with a puzzled frown.

"He does that sometimes." He held the K9's dark gaze, debating on whether he should reward the dog or not. Then he decided to go ahead. He didn't want Rocky to lose interest in the search for Eli game. "Good boy." He tossed the ball into the air.

Rocky caught it before it hit the floor.

"Is there anything you need before I start making calls?" he asked, shedding his coat, hat, and gloves. He removed the .38 from his pocket and set it on the end table. Then bent over to unlace his boots.

"Would you mind starting a fire?" Wyn still wore her

outer gear as she opened her laptop on the kitchen table. "I can't seem to get warm."

He suspected she wouldn't feel warm until they'd found Eli but went ahead and started the fire. Once he had a roaring blaze going, he pulled his phone from his pocket and sat on the sofa.

He'd expected to hear Doug's voice mail kick in, but a sleepy voice asked, "Chase? Is something wrong?"

"Sorry to wake you. And yeah, I need help." He filled Doug in on the missing child Eli Blackhorse and Rocky's search efforts over the past few hours. He didn't mention Eli being his son because he didn't want the conversation diverted off topic. The only thing that mattered was finding Eli.

The personal stuff would have to wait.

"Wow, you've done a good job in a short period of time," Doug said, sounding more awake. "Amazing how you were able to find that shell casing and the trailer house. You do realize, though, that I don't have jurisdiction on the rez."

"I know, but I was hoping your years of working in the federal government would help grease the wheels," he admitted. "I remember you met with the FBI agents in Cheyenne shortly after you found Emily."

"I did and will gladly give Special Agent in Charge Griffin Flannery a call," Doug said. "From what I've learned over the past two weeks, the feds delegate evidence collection to the state crime lab."

"But they're in Cheyenne, right?" The largest city in Wyoming happened to be located in the far southeast corner of the state. "The techs in Cody or Laramie are closer."

"I'll see what I can do," Doug promised. "Either city works for me, I've come to respect the crime scene techs that work out of Cody. They do a great job. Give me the location of the crime scene and I'll drag Griff out of bed."

"Thanks." He gave Doug the location as best he was able. "I don't know if I'll be able to meet your team there, depends on whether or not we get another lead."

"A missing kid should be a priority. I'm hoping I can get the techs deployed right away." Doug hesitated, then added, "Although I may get heat for the fact that you didn't call the feds in sooner."

"I'll take the blame." Chase wearily rubbed the back of his neck. "We've been following leads but have reached a dead end, at least for the moment. We're trying other options, but honestly, the sooner they can process the DNA from the beer bottles and check the shell casing, the better."

"Hear you on that. I'll be in touch." Doug ended the call, presumably to wake up the FBI agent in Cheyenne.

"Chase?" He jumped to his feet, turning to face Wynona. His sudden movement startled Rocky, who also jumped to his feet, then yawned as if annoyed he'd been woken from his nap. "I found the owner of the house, but it's a woman. A woman by the name of Julia Stone." She looked at him. "Do you think a woman could be behind this?"

"Anything is possible, but keep in mind she could also be related to the kidnappers in some way. A sister, mother, or grandmother." He crossed the room to join her at the kitchen table. Rocky followed, but then stretched out and lowered his head to go back to his napping. "Does she own other properties? Maybe she has a couple of sons, and they're living at different houses."

"No." Her slim shoulders deflated. "I don't see anything else listed under her name."

"Okay, what about other owners with the same last name of Stone?" He didn't want this to be the end of the trail. "She might be divorced. Or has a brother with the same last name."

"Let's see what I can find." Her fingers flew across the keyboard. Computer searches were not his area of expertise, his partner had created their wilderness hunting and fishing guide website. Chase had spent most of his life outdoors and preferred that over paperwork.

After their parents had been killed in the airplane crash, he and Maya discovered they were the executors of their estate. He'd been forced to learn how to navigate the legal system very quickly. Yet computer work still wasn't his strong suit.

"No other properties under the last name of Stone." Wyn looked dejected. "The only thing we know for sure is that she's registered with one of the Native American tribes. Only tribal members can own property on the rez."

"Social media?" He was at a loss as to how to help. "Maybe we can find a list of friends or relatives with another name?"

"Can't hurt," Wyn said as she went back to working the keyboard. "What do you think of calling the tribal police to let them know her house is a crime scene? Maybe they can issue an arrest warrant for her?"

"I'll call Doug back, have him search for vehicles registered to the name of Julia Stone." He hated bothering Doug again so soon. He called, but Doug didn't answer. Assuming his future brother-in-law was still on the phone with the feds, he left a quick message. "Hey, Doug, need help identifying the DMV registration of a woman named Julia Stone. Unknown DOB, but possibly mid-forties or fifties. Thanks."

Then he sat back to wait. As the room warmed from the fire, a wave of exhaustion hit hard. Without something constructive to work on, his body defaulted into resting mode. He shook his head to clear away the fatigue, then stood. "Do you mind if I make coffee?"

"Help yourself." Wyn didn't look up from the screen.

Rocky opened one eye, then closed it again. At times like this, he envied the dog's ability to fall asleep at the drop of a hat. He made the coffee, then racked his brain for another way to find Eli.

One thing was for sure, there were two kidnappers involved. Two sets of tire tracks meant one was driving something other than a white pickup truck.

The opportunities to find these guys were getting slim. If they didn't find something to break the case open, they may have little choice but to sit around and wait for the DNA results.

And what if their perp wasn't in the system?

Wynona abruptly stood and began to pace. "I can't find Julia Stone on social media." Her voice vibrated with frustration. "I found her in the tribal registry, but there aren't any siblings or children mentioned."

He frowned. "Could she be renting the place?"

"Yes, but I don't have access to those records." She whirled to face him. "But the feds may be able to dig into that, right?"

"I'll ask." He didn't like the case ending like this either. "I'm sure Doug will call me back soon."

She nodded, then turned away. When she wiped at her face, he realized she was crying.

"Don't give up, Wyn," he murmured, crossing over to put his arm around her shoulders. "Try to stay positive. To have faith. We're going to find him."

"Are we?" Her voice thickened with tears. She turned into his embrace, burying her face against his chest. "I can't stand it. We need to find him, Chase. I can't bear the thought of something happening to him. He's just a little boy!"

"I know." His resentment and anger morphed into empathy. He gathered her close, resting his hair on her dark silky hair, breathing in her unique scent. This wasn't the time to be at odds. They were stuck in this nightmare together.

And that meant leaning on each other until they had Eli home safe.

5

C linging to Chase, Wyn couldn't hold back her tears. Sobs ripped from her chest, her tears soaking Chase's thick denim shirt. Deep down, she agonized over the situation. Why was this happening? Who could be evil enough to do something like this? And why? There was no logical reason for her son to have been targeted by a masked man. He was an innocent boy who didn't deserve this.

Was the kidnapping a personal vendetta against her? She didn't want to believe that Eli had already been taken off the reservation and sold to some horrible child-trafficking ring. But the possibility was all too real.

Even worse, the hour was eleven at night. There wasn't anything more they could do to find Eli until morning.

"Please don't cry," Chase whispered, his voice near her ear. "We won't stop searching for Eli until we find him."

"How?" Her voice came out as a croak. She struggled to wrestle her tears under control, but it wasn't easy. "We don't know where to look!"

He didn't answer, just gathered her close and held her

tight. She welcomed his embrace. She hated to admit how desperately she needed Chase. His strength, his determination. His reassuring presence.

And of course, Rocky's keen ability to alert on Eli's scent. Without Chase and Rocky's expertise, they wouldn't know anything at all.

But they did know something. They had a trailer house owned by a woman by the name of Julia Stone.

She pulled herself together with an effort. But it wasn't easy. Eli wasn't like other kids. She had no idea how the little boy was handling the ordeal of being held by strangers.

Deep down, she knew she needed to let Chase know what to expect when, not if, but *when* they found Eli. There were many things to discuss, but Eli was the most important. Yet she was reluctant to leave the warmth of his arms.

"Let's sit on the sofa," Chase whispered. "Maybe we can come up with another avenue to explore in finding Eli."

She lifted her head and nodded. Breaking free of his embrace, she reached for the box of tissues on the table. Seeing them only made her want to cry again. She blew her nose and wiped her face. "I shouldn't have sent Eli to his preschool program. I knew he was coming down with a cold, but I sent him anyway." Her breath hitched, and she blew her nose again.

Chase searched her gaze. "Are you worried he'll get sicker? Will he run a fever and need additional medical care, like antibiotics?"

"It's not that. I don't think he'll need to be taken to the clinic." She drew in a deep breath, then moved past him to sit on the sofa. "I just hate knowing how much he may be suffering through this ordeal. Bad enough to feel sick, but even worse when strangers are holding you against your will. I don't see the men who took him being kind enough to offer any sort of comfort."

"Maybe they will." Chase settled beside her, resting his arm behind her on the sofa. "I wish I knew more about him."

That was her cue to tell him about their son. She glanced over as he pulled the phone from his pocket to stare down at the photograph she'd sent. Seeing Eli's unsmiling face brought fresh tears to her eyes. She tried to think of a way to ease into the subject. "Eli doesn't talk much, but he's smart. He understands everything, but he also gets easily preoccupied."

Chase frowned. "What do you mean? Was there a problem during his birth? Is he delayed in his growth and development?"

"No, he's not delayed. There were no problems during his birth." She tried to think of an easy way to tell him about their son's diagnosis. But before she could broach the subject, his phone rang.

"Hold that thought." Chase jumped to his feet and answering the call. "Hey, Doug. Do you have good news for me?"

When she couldn't hear the other side of his conversation, she waved to get Chase's attention. "Please put the call on speaker. I want to know what's going on."

He nodded. "Hold on, Doug. I'm going to put this on speaker so Wynona, she's Eli's mother, can hear." He lowered the phone, pressed the screen, then said, "Okay, go ahead. You said you spoke to FBI agent Flannery?"

"Yeah, sorry it took a while, he didn't answer right away, so I kept calling," Doug said. "He was irritated at first but understood the urgency when I explained what's happened. He's sending a team out to the trailer house at dawn."

She looked at her watch. Dawn was at least seven hours away. "Can they hit the road sooner so that they're here by the time it's light outside?"

"I suggested that approach," Doug admitted. "He said he'd try but wouldn't make any promises."

"What about asking the tribal police to stand guard over the residence to help preserve the evidence until the team can get here?" Chase asked. "I wish I had thought of making that call myself, but it just occurred to me now."

Doug sighed. "I suggested that, too, but it sounds as if that request isn't likely to be well received by the tribe. While the FBI has some authority over crimes that are committed on the reservation, the tribal police resent their interference. Sounded as if Griff didn't want to overstep any boundaries."

"A four-year-old's life is at stake!" She couldn't help lashing out anger. "I don't care if the tribal police get stomped on as long as Eli is found safe!"

"I understand," Doug said in a placating tone. "But don't worry, because I'm heading out soon to take on that job myself."

She glanced at Chase in surprise. He nodded and offered an encouraging smile. "Thanks, Doug. Like I said, I should have thought of it earlier. I'll head back to stand guard over the trailer until you can get there." He hesitated, then added, "I only returned to Wynona's house because someone fired a gun at us. Bullet sliced along the top of my snowmobile trailer."

"If that's the case, I'm not sure you should leave her alone," Doug said. "We don't know what type of criminal we're dealing with."

"I'll be fine," she said, even though the thought of staying there alone was nerve-racking. The shooting incident was still fresh in her mind. They also had no clue why Eli had been taken in the first place. No ransom. No nothing.

If the ultimate goal was to harm her, the kidnappers could make another attempt at any moment. She glanced out at the darkness. For all they knew, someone was watching her home now.

Yet she refused to do anything that might slow the investigation into Eli's disappearance. If that meant sitting here alone while Chase headed back to the trailer house, then fine. She'd manage.

"I'll leave Rocky here to keep an eye on things." Chase's voice broke into her thoughts. "He's not a trained attack dog, but he'll raise a ruckus if anyone gets too close. His bark can be quite intimidating."

"That's up to you," Doug said. "Just know I'm on my way. Oh, and I looked into the DMV database. There's nothing on Julia Stone. Either she doesn't have a car or she didn't bother to register it."

"Thanks for checking," Chase said. "It's disappointing, but maybe the feds can find something more."

"I hope so," Doug agreed.

She was touched by how quickly Chase's friend rallied around them. "Thanks, Doug. I'm grateful for everything you've done."

"As you pointed out, a child is missing," he said. "This is the least I can do."

"See you soon, then," Chase said. "Call when you're close. I know you're not familiar with the rez."

"Will do." Doug ended the call.

"How do you know him?" She eyed Chase curiously. "I don't remember a friend named Doug. Your business partner was Dave, right?"

"Right. Doug Bridges is a former DEA agent from Wisconsin. Last month, he asked my sister Maya for help in finding his half sister, Emily. Their mission was successful, and now Doug and Maya are engaged to be married." He held her gaze. "He's a great guy, and we're thrilled to have him become a part of our family."

Was there a hidden meaning to his words? Was he trying to tell her that she would have been welcome in his family too? But if so, why had he stayed away for so long? By the time so many weeks had passed, she'd stubbornly blocked his number to avoid him.

She was as much to blame as he was. Yet this wasn't the time to focus on the past. All that mattered was finding Eli. "I'm happy for Maya and Doug. He mentioned he works for the state now, but it sounds like his background has helped smooth things over with the FBI."

"Yes, he made a point of reaching out to them after finding the guys who took Emily. I'm sure Doug's experience will be helpful down the road too." Chase glanced down at Rocky who was stretched out on the floor near the fire, sleeping. "I'm going to drive back to the trailer house. I wasn't kidding about Rocky being a good guard dog. He isn't specifically trained to attack, but I'm confident he'll protect you."

"I have no doubt he can scare people away." She twisted her fingers together, trying to downplay her nervousness. "And I'm sure the kidnappers are long gone."

Chase frowned. "Maybe I'll take Rocky out and do a sweep of the area before I leave, just to be sure. It doesn't make sense that anyone would hang around, but it won't hurt to double-check."

It was on the tip of her tongue to offer to go with him, then she realized she needed to prove she wasn't afraid to be left alone. There was no point in telling him she was scared out of her mind because she didn't want to stand in his way. If he wanted to go watch over the evidence, then she would support him on that.

She forced a nonchalant smile. "Sounds good. Thanks."

Chase took a step toward her, then paused and turned away to grab his coat. When he had his coat and boots on, he called, "Come, Rocky."

The Elkhound shot upright, then rose to his four feet and meandered to Chase's side. As they left, she wondered if he'd been about to hug her again and wished he would have. She longed for the loving relationship they'd lost over five years ago.

After a particularly difficult argument with her father, she had sought shelter in Chase's arms. Despite knowing better, they'd given in to temptation and subsequently created Eli. She had battled shame and guilt after that night, especially when she'd realized she'd become pregnant. The day she'd discovered she was carrying Chase's child was the day his parents had been reported missing over the mountains and presumed dead. She should have told him, but she'd only been two months along and thought she should wait until he'd settled things with his siblings. That had taken a long time. Then her aunt had been diagnosed with end-stage cancer, so she'd gone to care for her father's sister.

The days became weeks, then a full month. She'd been too full of pride to reach out to Chase after hearing nothing from him during that entire time. The fact that her father strongly disliked Chase didn't help matters. She'd been torn between removing her child from his heritage and following her heart. She'd stubbornly held her silence.

Yet she had never forgotten him.

Now here they were, united in their efforts to find their

son. She should have called Chase. Should have told him the truth.

Would Eli be missing now if she had contacted Chase about her pregnancy? Alone in the house, she lowered herself onto the sofa and buried her face in her hands. No, she was certain her life and Eli's would have been very different if she hadn't allowed her pride to stand in her way. She should have tried to meet Chase halfway. Maybe gone out to the ranch to see him.

Eli's kidnapping may be God's punishment for her sins. Her son didn't deserve this agony, but she did.

She wasn't an expert on Chase's Christian faith, but she had a Bible tucked away in her dresser drawer. She didn't grab it now, but she closed her eyes and silently prayed for God to forgive her. To give her a second chance to be a better parent to Eli.

And most of all, to protect her son from harm.

FOR ONCE, Rocky stayed close to Chase's side as he strode down the street scanning their surroundings. The bitter cold air slapped at his face, and his breath caused puffs of steam to form. He strode quickly, hit by a sense of urgency. Rocky trotted to keep up. Maybe the K9 could sense his unease. He wasn't entirely convinced that leaving Wynona alone for several hours was the right thing to do.

Yet as he looked from one side of the neighborhood to the other, he didn't see anything unusual. Most of the houses were dark; only a few had a glow from a wood-burning stove. He caught the faint scent of burning wood as he passed by.

It didn't take long to make a loop around her neighborhood. He was struck by the haphazard locations of some of the houses. Some were on an angle; others were set really far off the road. Others were closer. They were not situated in neat rows the way most cities and towns were structured. The rez had its own rules.

Or rather, a lack of rules. There was no government overreach or specific city or state zoning laws. In some ways, it was great.

In others, not so much.

Returning to the rez after all this time was a painful reminder of the past. Not just his past relationship with Wynona, but their cultural differences. He couldn't help but feel guilty for the way his ancestors had treated Wynona's people. Not that he should feel the need to carry their sins as his own. Yet the truth was, the land was stolen from the Native Americans by force and violent bloodshed, reducing the proud men and women who once roamed the land to a square footage of land in the middle of Wyoming.

The eastern Shoshone and northern Arapaho tribes had been reduced to a fraction of the land they once roamed freely. Sure, big game had returned to the rez, but over the years, that hadn't helped. From what he could tell, the poverty and crime was worse than ever.

Young people were leaving the reservation in droves, searching for a better life for themselves and their families. Chase often wondered if there would be any Native Americans living here on the Wind River Reservation fifty years from now. He did not have high hopes for the tribe's ability to turn things around.

Yet he couldn't change the past. And neither could Wynona. Or her father, despite his obviously derogatory feelings for the white man, as he'd referred to Chase.

"Go and leave my daughter alone!" The old man had thun-

dered at him. His face had turned so red Chase had been
concerned about his health. "Leave now, White Man! You have no
business here."

Chase had left, but now he realized he shouldn't have
caved under the old tribesman's tactics. He should have
stayed and fought for Wynona.

Then Kendra had called, sobbing about how she was
certain their parents' death wasn't an accident, that the
plane crash had been intentional. She begged Chase to keep
looking for them.

So he'd turned his back on Ogima and Wynona
Blackhorse and left the Wind River Reservation. Sacrificing
Wynona for his family.

Only he hadn't realized he was giving up his son too.
Never in a million years would he have done that.

Six months ago, he'd failed to find Alecia alive. Now he
was back, searching for a son he'd never met. He'd missed
out on the first four years of Eli's life. And if they didn't find
Eli soon, he might never be given the opportunity to know
his son.

He glanced up at the starless sky, silently asking for
God's help, then turned his attention back to his surroundings. He glanced at Rocky who stood sniffing the air, his ears
pricked. "Get busy."

The dog just stood there, looking at him. With a sigh, he
headed up to Wyn's front door. "Fine, have it your way," he
said to the dog.

As if to prove his independence, Rocky strode toward a
scrubby bush and lifted his leg. Chase tried the door, but it
was locked.

"Wynona?" He rapped on the wood. "It's Chase."

The door swung open. "You're back." She looked
relieved.

Rocky bounded forward, brushing past him to go inside. Chase stepped over the threshold, closing the door behind him. "Rocky and I did a sweep of the area and didn't find anything alarming. Your neighbors are tucked in for the night as far as I can tell."

"They usually are at this hour mid-workweek." She crossed her arms over her chest, offering a crooked smile. "I appreciate you checking to make sure everything is fine. I don't mind being here with Rocky."

"You're sure?" He fought the urge to pull her into his arms by patting Rocky's fluffy head instead. "If something happens, call me. I'll take the SUV without the added weight of the trailer, so I can be back here in a matter of minutes."

"Nothing will happen." She gestured to the laptop computer. "I'll stay busy by continuing to search for information on Julia Stone."

He nodded. "Do you mind if I take coffee to go?"

"Of course not, help yourself." She knelt beside Rocky, running her fingers through his fluffy hair. "You're going to be a good boy for me, aren't you?"

Rocky nudged her with his nose, making her smile. But the brief flash of humor quickly vanished as she stood.

He filled a mug with coffee and headed for the door. Out of nowhere, Rocky rose to his feet and began to howl, a high-pitched baying sound only a hound could make.

"What in the world?" Wynona's eyes were wide. "Why is he doing that?"

"I'm not sure." He set the coffee aside. "What's wrong, Rock?"

The dog crossed to the window and howled again. Then he spun and ran toward the front door.

"Maybe he needs to—how did you say it? Get busy?" Wyn said.

"No, that's not it." He stared at the dog for a moment. Rocky looked back at him as if willing Chase to read his mind. He reached over to open the front door. Rocky instantly bolted forward, going back outside. Concerned, he followed, trying to figure out what had caught his K9's attention.

An intruder? He'd just walked the area, so he didn't see how that was possible.

Rocky stood in the road and lifted his nose to the air. He let out another musical howl, as if determined to wake the entire neighborhood.

And maybe that's exactly what his dog wanted. Chase abruptly realized the smoke scent in the air was stronger now. Obviously, many of the homes on the rez had wood-burning stoves and fireplaces like Wynona's, but he didn't believe that was the source of the scent. The pungent smell that wafted toward him now was different. Heavier. Thicker and not as clean smelling.

Had the wind shifted?

He turned in a circle until he caught a glimpse of an eerily orange glow in the distance. He narrowed his gaze, realizing it was north and slightly west of his current location.

A fire! He knew the fire was what caught Rocky's attention. Wild animals were always in tune to their surroundings and would run fast and furiously from a fire. His Elkhound had years of instincts bred into him.

Chase abruptly spun toward his SUV and trailer. As he worked to disconnect the trailer from his vehicle, Wynona joined him. Beside her was Rocky, who had finally stopped howling.

"What's burning?" she asked.

"I'm not sure. But you can see the blaze from here." He didn't want to voice his concern, but he worked faster on disconnecting the trailer hitch. He didn't have his flashlight handy, and it wasn't easy to unhook the lighting mechanism in the dark. "I'll find out and call you with an update once I know more."

"If that's a fire, then I'm coming with you." Wyn's voice was firm. "I'll call for help along the way."

There wasn't time to argue. He finally had the trailer disconnected from the SUV. He shoved it backward, then opened the rear hatch for Rocky. The dog jumped inside without hesitation, as if sensing time was of the essence.

Seconds later, he was driving toward the orange glow. Now that he was in the driver's seat, he could see a hazy plume of smoke rising into the sky. The burning scent grew stronger, and he belatedly realized he should have rewarded Rocky for alerting them to the fire.

Next time, not that he wanted there to be another fire. He wished he'd have paid more attention to the smoky scent earlier. He'd assumed fireplaces and stoves.

Not a burning building.

As he navigated one street to the next, the ball of dread in his gut grew.

"Chase?" Wyn's voice was a hoarse whisper. "What if the source of the fire is the trailer house where Rocky alerted on Eli's scent?"

"It could be any house," he said, although he, too, had a bad feeling about this. Fires didn't just randomly start in the middle of winter.

She used her phone to call the tribal police to notify them of the fire. "Yes, I understand. Thank you." She lowered the phone. "They're notifying the volunteer fire department here in Riverton to respond."

"I'm glad the city has a fire department," Chase said. "I wasn't sure those services were even available."

"They're 100 percent volunteer," she said. "They'll get assistance from the Fort Washakie's paid fire department if needed, but that's thirty to forty minutes away." She turned to look at him. "I'm worried, Chase. I don't think this fire is an accident. I'm afraid it was set on purpose."

"I'm concerned too." He kicked himself for not staying at the scene of the crime right from the start. How long had it been since they'd left the place? Thirty minutes? No, closer to an hour by the time they walked back. Then he'd called Doug, comforted Wyn, and then walked around the neighborhood as if he'd had all the time in the world.

Now they might be too late.

He hit the gas, sending the SUV surging forward. He took the turns at a dangerous speed, slowing only when they reached the location of the fire.

The flames were blinding in their brightness. And from what he could see, the entire house was engulfed in flames.

"It is!" Wyn cried. "It's the trailer house!"

Yanking the wheel, he pulled off to the side of the road to avoid blocking access from the volunteer firefighters. He shot out of the car, heading toward the house. He couldn't get very close because the blaze was too hot.

Even as he stood there, he knew with sick certainty that it was a lost cause. The DNA evidence left behind by Eli's kidnapper had been destroyed.

And he had no one to blame but himself.

6

W ynona stared in shock. It was gone. The trailer. The beer bottle evidence. The only link to the people who had taken her son.

Gone!

"I'm sorry." Chase's low voice vibrated with regret. "I should have stayed here. I never should have left. Now it's too late."

"How did they know we were here?" She couldn't tear her eyes from the blaze. "How did they know to get rid of the trailer?"

"I'm not sure." Chase's expression was grim. "It's possible one of them came back in time to see Rocky. I should have insisted we call the tribal police when Rocky alerted on Eli's scent."

A shiver that had nothing to do with the freezing temperature ran down her spine. Setting the fire to eliminate evidence was deliberately sinister. And she was horrified to know the same people who'd done this also had her son.

"We need to get out of here." Chase's tone turned urgent. "Whoever started this fire could still be in the area."

"Can we try to find him?" As she voiced the question, she knew the answer. Chase would never risk his K9. And she wouldn't ask him to. "Never mind. I just hate knowing we're back to square one."

Chase gripped her arm, tugging her toward the SUV. "No, we can't search in the darkness. Not while knowing this guy is armed and dangerous. Besides, I need to call Doug. I'm not sure there's a good reason for the feds to send a crime scene team out now."

Swallowing hard, she hurried back to the SUV. She caught the reflection of the fire in Rocky's eyes before sliding into the passenger seat. Before Chase even got in the driver's side, the SUV rumbled to life. The sound of the engine startled her, but then she remembered Chase mentioning something about how the vehicle was specially designed for his dog.

The minute Chase was seated, he made the call.

"Hey, Chase, I'm still an hour and forty-five minutes out," Doug said.

"The trailer house is on fire," Chase said bluntly. "The evidence is being destroyed as we speak."

There was a long silence as Doug digested that information. "Not good," he finally said.

"It's my fault." Chase shook his head. "I should have considered the possibility they'd do something like this."

"You were never a cop, Chase," Doug pointed out. "Besides, if you had been there, you may have been killed."

That thought hadn't occurred to her. Wyn shivered again. "Can DNA still be taken from beer bottles that have been burned in a fire?"

"Maybe," Doug said. "Typically a house fire would not

burn hot enough to melt a glass bottle. But if the same guys who kidnapped your son returned to get rid of the evidence, we should assume they took the beer bottles with them."

Another depressing possibility that hadn't occurred to her. "I guess we'll find out once the fire is out. And Chase still has the shell casing."

"That's better than nothing," Doug agreed.

The shrill of sirens filled the night air. Hearing them, Rocky lifted his head and howled. She turned to look at the K9. "Does he always do that?"

"Yep." Chase shrugged. "I think it's a hound thing. Some sort of instinct inbred in his doggy DNA."

She nodded, impressed that the volunteer firefighters had mobilized so quickly. They obviously took their role seriously. And their fast response gave her a bit of hope. Maybe if they could get the fire under control relatively quickly, they could salvage something from the wreckage.

"Doug, you should probably turn around and head back to the ranch." Chase spoke over the dual sounds of Rocky howling and the sirens. "There isn't anything you can do here."

"Are you sure?" Doug sounded uncertain.

"I'm sure," Chase said. "Fact is, I may need Maya and some of the other siblings to head over to help if we learn anything new. For now, you should stick close to the ranch. If the situation changes, you and the others will be the first to know."

"Okay, then," Doug agreed. "We're ready if you need us."

"I know, and I'm grateful to have your expertise." Chase glanced at her. "Thanks, Doug."

He ended the call, then slowly rolled past the house fire. Behind them, swirling red and white lights announced the arrival of the fire engine. Using the side mirror, she watched as the fire truck and a large water truck parked near the property. Rocky fell silent once the sirens stopped. Several firefighters emerged from the rig and began uncoiling hoses.

The fire was in their hands now. Her stomach churned with nausea, but she tried to ignore it. "I need to keep working the Julia Stone angle. She must be related to the kidnappers or at least have rented the house to them. She must know their names and contact information."

"I agree." He didn't say anything else for a long moment. "You have every right to blame me for this."

"What?" She'd been thinking about other avenues she could use to dig into Julia Stone. "Why would I blame you?"

"If I'd been thinking like a cop . . ." He didn't finish. There was a long pause before he continued. "I figured the kidnappers were long gone, especially after taking shots at us. I never considered the possibility they'd come back to clean up their mess."

"I didn't think of that either." She lightly touched his arm. "It's not your fault. All we can do is to hope that the FBI can still get some DNA from the beer bottles. If they're inside." She tried to smile. "Maybe the kidnappers started the fire assuming the bottles would burn. They may not realize that DNA could still be obtained from them."

He nodded, but his expression didn't lighten with hope. "I hate knowing I failed. That I may never get a chance to meet my son."

His words hit hard. "Eli is not going to die," she said hotly. "He won't. We'll find him."

"Yes, of course. You're right." He took off his glove and reached for her hand, gently squeezing it. "I'm sorry. We need to stay positive."

She gripped his fingers tightly. "I'm sorry I didn't call you when I discovered I was pregnant. I mean, that was also the night your parents' plane crashed. But later, I should have called."

He nodded. "I share some of that blame. We spent weeks searching the mountain for my parents' plane and their bodies. We never found them." He sighed. "But let's not rehash the past now. I'd rather we keep pushing forward to find Eli."

She was touched by his comment, knowing he was being much nicer than she deserved. "Okay. But when we find him . . ."

"We'll talk," he finished for her. "And you should know I'm not giving up my son. Whatever arrangements we make will include him staying with me for at least half if not more of the time."

The knot in her stomach tightened, but she forced a nod. Because she'd known this would be the consequence the moment she called Chase for help. And watching how Chase and Rocky worked to find Eli, she'd known how wrong she'd been to keep their son from him.

Eli wasn't like other kids, but she knew the boy would benefit from having a strong father figure in his life. Her father had done his best to fill that gap, but being an indulgent grandparent was not the same.

She was about to fill Chase in on Eli's diagnosis when his phone rang. Doug Bridges's name flashed on the screen of the center console.

"What's up, Doug?" Chase asked.

"I gave FBI Agent Griff Flannery an update on the fire," Doug said. "I wanted you to know he still plans to bring the team up from Cheyenne in the morning to see what's left of the crime scene. And he's anxious to get that shell casing too."

"That's good to hear," Chase said. "I still feel bad that I didn't stick around to protect the place."

"Don't beat yourself up," Doug said. "Maybe they left other evidence behind by starting the fire. Oh, and that reminds me, Griff wanted to know if you've looped in the tribal police on this latest incident."

"I didn't, but we'll do that now." Chase glanced at her. She nodded and reached for her phone. "Thanks again."

"Anytime. Call when you have more intel. We'll be waiting."

"Will do. Thanks." Chase used his thumb to end the call.

She scrolled through her phone to contact the tribal police. Something she should have thought to do the minute they saw the fire.

Yet deep down, she knew that if anyone had a chance of finding Eli, it was Chase and his K9, Rocky.

All they needed was a general location to perform the search. She silently begged God to guide them in the right direction.

For Eli's sake.

ELI AWOKE to Smelly Man carrying him into a house. He held himself perfectly still, worried that the smelly man would drop him if he squirmed. He flinched when the smelly man kicked the door. "Come on, open up!"

The door opened, and Eli wasn't surprised to see Scary Man standing there, scowling at them. "Where have you been?"

"Hey, you're the one who told me to drive around for a while," Smelly Man said. Eli was taken into the house and set down on the sofa. "So that's what we did. We also ate some pizza for dinner. I've got leftovers in the truck if you're hungry."

Eli had been glad to be given a slice of cheese pizza. His stomach didn't hurt as much now that he'd eaten. But he was tired. He'd fallen asleep in the car. Now that he was awake, he put his hands into his pockets. He found his black horsey, but not the block. The block was missing!

He frantically looked around to see if he'd dropped the building block on the floor. He didn't see it. Was it still in the car? He didn't think so because it had been in his coat pocket.

Soft. Soft. Soft.

He began to rock, wishing desperately that he still had the building block. He felt lopsided, as if he couldn't sit up straight. He needed to have both items in his pockets.

Now he only had one.

Soft. Soft. Soft.

"Knock it off with the rocking." Smelly Man sounded crabby. "You're bugging me. Go to sleep already."

Eli didn't stop rocking, because he couldn't. He didn't have his block. He didn't have the hard toy to squeeze in his hand after the stuffed horse.

Soft. Soft. Soft. Eli's nose ran, and he swiped his arm over his face. His mom needed to hurry up and get there.

He didn't want to be with these two men anymore.

CHASE DID his best to push past the guilt over his failure to focus on their next steps. One thing that had occurred to him was that if the kidnappers had turned around to come back, they hadn't gone too far.

He wanted to believe they still had Eli here in Riverton.

Of all the cities within the rez, this was one of the larger ones. Maybe they thought they could blend in better here, considering they had a small child with them, than in another remote location.

And if that was the case, maybe he could look at a map and identify a few possible places they could be hiding.

He drove around the snowmobile trailer to pull in and park in Wynona's driveway. She quickly scrambled out of the passenger seat, clearly intending to get back to work on finding Julia Stone as fast as possible.

After releasing the back hatch, he got out too. He had a trailer lock in the back of the SUV and decided to put it on. It wasn't so much that he was worried about the cost of replacing the sleds, but more that he wanted them safe in case they needed to use them.

Rocky trotted around the front yard, lifting his leg in various spots. Chase kept an eye on the K9 as he dug the lock from the enclosure beneath Rocky's crate area.

He slipped the lock in place, straightened and headed to the house. After a moment's hesitation, Rocky joined him.

There was a chill in the air. He noticed the logs in the fireplace had collapsed into glowing coals. Seeing them made him think about the trailer house and what would be left once the fire had been doused.

Crossing to the fireplace, he added more logs and kindling, bringing the blaze to life. Then he shrugged out of his coat, hat, and gloves. For now, he kept his boots on.

Rocky stretched out in front of the fire and promptly fell asleep.

He bent, stroked a hand over his K9's soft fur, then turned to see Wyn sitting at the kitchen table in front of her computer. Her face was pale, and dark circles smudged the skin beneath her dark eyes. She needed sleep.

They both did.

But he knew that even suggesting such a thing would be considered a betrayal. In truth, he felt the same way. Yet this case was different enough from Alecia's that he tried to tell himself the outcome would be different too.

Better. That they'd find Eli alive and well.

He sighed and crossed over to join her. "I'll make more coffee."

"That's fine." She suddenly turned to look at him. "Would Doug have the ability to find more information on Julia Stone?"

"I'll ask." He figured Doug was probably pulling into the long winding driveway leading to the main ranch house and Maya's individual cabin. Thankfully, his sister's fiancé answered on the first ring. "Doug, I told you before that a woman by the name of Julia Stone owns the trailer house that was started on fire. And so far, we can't seem to find anything else about her. You said yourself that she's not in the DMV database. Do you think the feds could dig into her a bit? Maybe they have someplace to look for her that we've missed?"

"I can ask. I also have a tech expert I used to work with back in Milwaukee that I can try to contact," Doug said. "The problem is that they're an hour ahead of us. I don't know that he'll answer his phone now, as it's going on one in the morning there. Ian Dunlap may call me back at five or six in the morning his time."

"Anything you can do to help is appreciated," Chase said. "Her name is Julia Stone. We know she's of Native American heritage as she's listed in the tribal registry. But that's about all we know. We don't have an age, marital status, offspring, or siblings. We've got nothing to go on."

"This could be tricky," Doug said warily. "The feds keep

a hands-off approach when it comes to the Native Americans' personal lives."

That was exactly what he was afraid of. "Wynona has been searching social media but hasn't found her yet."

"Ian has been playing around with using DNA sites to help find suspects," Doug said. "Apparently, lots of people go on these sites and build family trees. Could be that one of those mentions Julia Stone."

It sounded like an extremely remote possibility, but he wasn't going to argue. "Can't hurt to try."

"Hang in there," Doug said. "And get some sleep. You need to be rested in case we get a lead early tomorrow morning."

"We'll try. Thanks again." He lowered the phone. "He's going to reach out to a tech expert he worked with back in Milwaukee. They're an hour ahead of us, so he'll talk to Ian early in the morning."

"Okay." Her haunted eyes stabbed deep into his heart. "I don't think Julia has a family, though, or they'd be listed within the tribal registry. Everyone living on the tribe gets a share of the profits from the casino. It's not much." Wyn dragged her fingers through her long, straight hair. "But it's enough that they'd register to get their fair share."

He knew the casino proceeds were shared with those living on the reservation, but he'd never asked for any details. "Maybe her parents are dead, but she has cousins or other relatives. She may have a sibling under a different name."

She nodded slowly. "I feel like this is taking too long. That we don't have time to waste waiting for the FBI or Ian to do their thing."

"I know." He went into the kitchen to start over with the pot of coffee. "Can you bring up a map of Riverton? I'd like to take a closer look at the area surrounding the trailer house."

"Sure." She worked the computer keyboard as he filled the coffee maker. "The trailer house is located on the outskirts of the city. The nicer homes tend to be closer to the Wind River and the hills overlooking the bison."

"I didn't see the bison, although I know they're out there." He finished the coffee and came to sit beside her. "I'm just curious if there's another set of trailer homes that are similar to that one."

"There are trailer homes all over." She frowned. "Besides, just because they kept Eli in the one trailer home doesn't mean the next one will be the same setup."

She was right about that, but he still wanted to see the area himself. Once she had the trailer house pinpointed on a map, he turned the computer toward him and began to zoom out.

Wyn propped her chin on her hand and leaned forward to watch. He manipulated the screen, trying to decide whether it was worth heading out with Rocky to do a search, when he noticed she swayed a bit. "Hey, are you okay?"

She nodded and yawned. Her body was clearly exhausted and craved rest. If he were being honest, his did too.

"We've been on an adrenaline roller coaster since this started," he said softly. "We can't keep going like this for long. You should stretch out on the sofa for an hour or so. We'll need all our strength and endurance to search for Eli come morning."

"No. I can't." She gently slapped her cheeks to wake herself up. "I'm fine. I'd rather we figure out a way to find Eli tonight."

"Technically, it's already morning." The coffee maker

sputtered, indicating it was finished brewing. He rose to his feet, filled two mugs, and brought them back. The coffee was strong and black, the way he liked it.

But if he had been hoping for a jolt of caffeine to hit his system, he was sorely disappointed.

He blinked to bring the screen into focus. Now that he was looking at the map, he realized his idea was likely a bust. There were far too many possibilities for Rocky to search for Eli's scent. As much as his dog loved the snow, he couldn't expose the K9 to the elements for too long. Dogs became dehydrated when sniffing and tracking for an extended length of time.

He was also worried that if the kidnappers had carried the kid around, Rocky may not hit on the little boy's scent at all. Wyn had mentioned the kid's runny nose, which may help. But only if he'd been outside for a while.

Staring at the map, he identified a few possibilities, but he knew the chances of finding Eli there were slim. Not to mention, it would be more dangerous to continue the search in the dark.

They were stuck, with nothing new to go on. He finished his coffee, then sat back in his chair. Glancing at Wyn, he smiled when he realized her eyes were closed, her chin dropping to her chest.

"Wyn." Her head jerked up when he said her name. He put a hand on her arm. "Come on, we need to get some rest."

"I—" She halted her immediate protest. "Okay," she reluctantly relented. "But it seems wrong to be sleeping when Eli is scared and lonely."

"By this hour, I'm sure Eli is sleeping." At least he hoped the child was resting. "We know they've moved locations once already. I doubt they'll head out again anytime soon."

She scrubbed her hands over her face, then rose to her feet. "I'll sleep in Eli's bed. You can use mine or the sofa. Whatever you'd like."

He nodded, understanding her need to be as close to their son as possible. "Okay. I'll sleep on the sofa."

She turned away, heading toward the bedrooms. He stayed where he was, watching as she turned into the first room on the right.

Chase bent to feed more wood into the fire, and Rocky opened his eyes for a brief moment, then closed them again with a heavy sigh. The dog was tired too. He stroked a hand over Rocky's fur, then finished with the fire.

Finally, he bent over to take his boots off. He stretched out on the sofa and closed his eyes. He'd expected to fall instantly asleep.

He didn't. He pulled his phone out, making sure the ringer was on so he'd wake up if Doug or anyone else called. Then he took a moment to pull up Eli's picture.

His son. He wished he'd done things differently five years ago. But at the time, the crisis of losing both parents in a small plane crash had consumed his time and energy.

He set his phone on his chest, closed his eyes, and prayed for forgiveness, for mercy, and for his son's safety.

A strange sound woke him a few minutes later. He bolted upright, confused about where he was. Then he realized the fire was almost out and that the noise was coming from the hallway leading to the bedrooms.

Not five minutes, but four hours. He rose to his feet and staggered toward the hallway. Rocky ignored him. As he drew closer, he could hear Wynona's harsh, heartbreaking sobs.

"Hey, don't cry. Please don't cry." He entered the room and found her crushing Eli's pillow to her chest. Sitting on the edge of the bed, he drew her into his arms. "We're going to find him."

"I—I had a nightmare," she said between hiccuping sobs. She wiped her face on the pillow, then looked up at him. "I heard Eli's voice asking me to come and get him, but the men holding him yelled at him to shut up, so he began to cry."

He could imagine the scenario all too well. He didn't have a lot of experience with small kids, but he knew they could get cranky and irritable. If Eli annoyed his captors, they could lash out at him verbally or physically. The thought made him wince.

He pulled her close. "I'm sure Eli is still sleeping."

"I—know." She struggled to get her emotions in check. "It's not like he's talking their ears off or anything."

He frowned, leaning back to see her eyes. "Are you saying Eli can't talk?"

"No, he can talk. When he wants to." She looked away, sighed, then added, "But he tends to be quiet."

"That doesn't sound like any of the kids I've ever seen." He was getting the sense she was holding something back. "I noticed he wasn't smiling in his picture."

"No. I—was going to tell you this earlier, but Eli has been diagnosed as autistic." She still wouldn't meet his gaze. "He's very smart but gets hyperfocused on odd things. Contrasts in particular. And he doesn't talk much. That's something we've been working on with Shana, his preschool teacher."

"Autistic?" he repeated, stunned. "Will his condition somehow impact his kidnappers? Will they get angry at him?"

"I doubt it." She finally met his gaze. "He's a quiet child, which should work in his favor. Even though he called out to me in my dream, I'm sure he hasn't spoken much while being with the strange men." She hesitated, and added, "You'll have to give him time to get used to you, Chase. He doesn't do well with change."

Chase realized his preconceived ideas about his first meeting with his son were way off base. From what Wyn was describing, his son wouldn't be happy to meet him.

Quite the opposite. More likely the little boy would be frightened of him.

His own father.

7

The stricken expression in Chase's eyes made her wince. She should have prepared him better, but their priority had been to find Eli. A task they had yet to accomplish.

Fresh tears threatened when she thought of her dream. Eli lifting his head and asking her to come and get him. She ached to hold her son close. Wanted desperately to find him safe and unharmed.

"Is Eli's diagnosis the reason you didn't call me?" Chase asked.

"What? No." She shook her head. "I didn't know his diagnosis until he was in for his two-year-old doctor visit. He was also so quiet. I was afraid his language skills were lagging behind. Yet when he did talk, he pronounced most words correctly. He just chooses not to talk much." She wasn't explaining it well. "The biggest concern now is that he doesn't interact with other kids or adults the way he should. He's rather withdrawn and retreats into his own world."

Chase's blue eyes bored into hers. "Has he been seen by a specialist?"

"Yes, I took him to Laramie." She knew where this was going. "The doctor recommended speech and physical therapy. And I took him to a few sessions, but he doesn't do well with strangers. After the first two weeks, I knew it would take Eli months of sessions to make any headway. I decided it was better to work with Shana his preschool teacher on the strategies they suggested." She lifted a hand when he opened his mouth. "Don't. Shana has been making good progress. Eli likes her. I can't just up and move him to another new home. Eli needs stability first and foremost." She paused, then added, "Especially after this."

"I understand what you're telling me. I have no desire to hurt Eli, but I still plan to be a part of his life." Chase's jaw was set at a stubborn angle. In a flash, she was reminded of Eli's expression when he didn't want to do something. She hadn't realized how her son had inherited several of Chase's traits. Something she hadn't fully appreciated until now.

"I know that," she said mildly. "You just need to understand that it will take time. You can't expect Eli to welcome you with open arms."

There was a long moment before Chase reluctantly nodded. "He can have all the time he needs. I'm not going to give up. But for now, we need to find him. Knowing this, I'm worried the kidnappers will get frustrated with him."

"I doubt having a quiet kid will annoy them," she said. "It's the one sliver of hope that I've been holding on to. I once told Eli that being quiet was his superpower. I wanted him to know that being quiet isn't necessarily a bad thing. I encourage him to tell me with words what he needs, but I also reassure him that it's okay to be the way he is. To have has his own way of processing the world around us."

"Is autism common within Native American tribes?" Chase asked.

"No. In fact, there are less cases of autism reported within the Native American communities. Although that could be in part because the condition is underdiagnosed. Many Native Americans don't accept western health practices." She held his gaze in the darkness. "I've also been told the disease can be genetic."

Another long silence as he processed that information. Then Chase stood and raked his hand through his chocolate-brown hair. His jaw was shadowed as he hadn't shaved since yesterday. She rather liked him that way. "Okay. Thanks for telling me."

He turned and left Eli's bedroom. Knowing that trying to sleep would be futile, she set her son's pillow aside and headed into the bathroom. Feeling gritty, she showered, changed, and let her hair air dry. Then she walked into the kitchen.

A pot of coffee was brewing, the third in less than five hours, she thought wearily. Maybe now that they'd gotten a little sleep, they could focus on their next steps.

She noticed Chase had already been outside with Rocky. The dog sat and stared up at Chase as he stood beside a set of dog dishes he must have gotten from his SUV. The food dish was full, but Rocky had apparently not been given permission to eat.

"Good boy," Chase finally said. He made a hand gesture, pointing toward the dish of food. "Go get it."

Rocky stared at him for another heartbeat, then moved forward to begin eating. She gestured toward the K9. "He's very well trained."

"He is. Although he tends to balk at taking orders." Chase offered a crooked smile. "He's not like Maya's Zion or

Jessica's Belgian sheepdog, Teddy. They follow their handlers around, eager to please. Rocky is independent and views the search game as a challenge rather than a desire to make me happy."

"I didn't realize dogs could each have such different personalities." She crossed to the fridge. "I'll find something to make breakfast."

"Thanks." Chase returned to his seat in front of the computer. She knew he was likely reviewing the map of the location around the trailer home. The hour was ten minutes past six o'clock in the morning. She hoped Eli was still sleeping because she couldn't bear the thought of the kidnappers not feeding him breakfast.

She pulled eggs, ham, and cheese from the fridge and glanced over at him. "Are omelets okay?"

"Perfect." He didn't look away from the screen. "I texted Doug; he's waiting to hear back from his tech expert back in Milwaukee. I want to have some properties for Ian to examine more closely."

"I understand, but he won't have access to the tribal housing database." She broke eggs into a bowl and began to whisk them together. "I can find the names of property owners, but I don't know how that helps us."

"I'm hoping Ian can get a line on Julia Stone," he said. "Once we have a few names of friends or relatives, I'll ask you to check the housing database to see if any of them live close enough to be involved."

She nodded, belatedly remembering their conversation from earlier that morning. As much as she hadn't wanted to sleep, she had to admit she felt better having logged a few hours of rest.

As she diced the ham, she silently vowed that today was the day. They'd find Eli and bring him home.

They had to. She couldn't stand the possibility of another day going by without locating her son.

By the time she had prepared their ham and cheese omelets, Chase's phone still hadn't rung with any news. She carried the plates to the table, then reached for the coffee pot to refill their cups.

"This looks amazing, thanks," Chase said with a smile.

"No problem." She folded her hands in her lap. "If you don't mind, I'd like you to say grace."

He raised a brow but didn't hesitate. "Of course." He reached for her hand. As his warm fingers closed around hers, she was keenly aware of the sizzle of awareness. Totally inappropriate reaction considering Eli was missing, so she lowered her head to hide her expression. "Dear Lord Jesus, we thank You for this food we are about to eat. We ask You to keep our son, Elijah, safe in Your care. Please grant us the strength and wisdom we need to find him. Amen."

"Amen." Her voice hitched, and she swallowed hard. "Thanks, Chase. I needed to hear that."

"Always." He continued to hold her hand. "You're not alone in this, Wyn."

"I know." She managed a wan smile. Somehow, she felt closer to Chase this morning. Maybe because they were in this together. And he knew everything about Eli. "How did you know that Eli's full name is Elijah?"

"Because it's from the Bible." He finally released her to pick up his fork. "As soon as you called him Eli, I knew you hadn't given up your faith."

She hadn't. "I've attended church here a few times, although not as often as I should."

"We often hold Sunday morning services on the ranch during the winter," Chase said. "Between the forty-five-minute drive to Cody and the unpredictable weather, it's easier. We don't do anything formal. We tend to take turns reading passages from the Bible."

"That sounds nice." She had no concept of what his life was like while living on the ranch. In some ways, the Chase she knew had been replaced with a different version of him. A more solemn, mature version.

As if reading her thoughts, he said, "I've had to take on the role of father figure to our younger siblings. That first year was rough, but things have gotten better over time."

"I can imagine." Was that his way of apologizing for not coming to find her? "I only met your parents once at Thanksgiving, and they were wonderful to me."

"They were role models in every way." His voice was low and husky. "We miss them terribly, but I know they are up in heaven watching over us." The corner of his mouth tipped upward. "And I'm sure they approve of the changes we've made to the ranch. Especially the new K9 search and rescue services we provide."

She nodded in agreement. It was an honorable mission. She needed every bit of Chase's and Rocky's expertise.

Her appetite had vanished, but she forced herself to eat. She needed to believe Eli would be eating breakfast soon too.

Please, Lord, please keep our son safe in Your care!

ELI AWOKE at the sound of something banging loudly. Instantly, he remembered everything. The smelly man and the scary man taking him from Miss Shana's house. The way they'd driven around for a while, then went to the one house. Leaving that house to drive around again to end up here. Even the cheese pizza Smelly Man had given him.

He was hungry. If he was at home, his mom would instruct him to use his words. To tell her, "Mom, I'm hungry." But here, he didn't dare speak out loud. He sat up on the sofa, eyeing the smelly man as he banged around in the kitchen, muttering under his breath.

"There had better be some food in this place," Smelly Man said. "I'm not running out to get breakfast."

Glancing down at the sofa, Eli spotted his stuffed horsey. He reached for it, squeezing it gently.

Soft. Soft. Soft.

The words echoed hollowly in his mind. It wasn't the same without the building block. He felt off balance, as if he were sitting lopsided. He began to rock back and forth, trying not to cry.

Soft. Soft. Soft.

He wondered if the building block was in the car? Maybe it had fallen from his pocket and was stuck in the crack between the seats. He considered using his words to ask Smelly Man if he could go outside to check. He really wanted his block back.

"There you are," Smelly Man said to the scary man when he entered the kitchen. "There isn't much food here."

"So what?" Scary Man sounded crabby. Eli called him scary because he'd worn the face mask when he'd come into Miss Shana's house. Without the mask, he could have been Crabby Man. But he would still be scary. "You're always yammering on about food. What's with that?"

"I'm hungry," Smelly Man said. "I wanna eat."

"We gotta leave again soon anyway," Scary Man said. "We'll grab something on the way."

"Why do we have to move?" Smelly Man complained. "We just got here late last night. Nobody even saw us come inside."

"Because the boss wants us to, that's why." Scary Man jabbed his finger into Smelly Man's chest. "Don't argue. Just do as you're told."

There was a moment of silence as the two men stared at each other. Eli worried they might start fighting. If they did, could he run away?

"Fine!" Smelly Man threw his hands into the air. "But I want breakfast from that fast-food restaurant down the road."

"Whatever." Scary Man looked over to see Eli watching them. His expression turned dark. "What are you staring at, kid?"

Eli quickly dropped his gaze to his lap. He rocked back and forth faster this time. Back. Forth. Back. Forth. Backforthbackforth.

"Get your coat on, kid," Smelly Man said.

Eli calmed himself and reached for his coat. He'd thought his mommy would have come for him by now. Maybe now that it was morning, she'd continue searching for him.

He blinked and sniffled loudly. His nose was still running. And he was hungry.

The only good thing was that he could search for his block when he was in the back seat of the truck.

AFTER FINISHING HIS BREAKFAST, Chase carried his dirty dishes to the sink. He'd noticed there was no dishwasher in Wynona's home and began filling the sink with warm, sudsy water.

"I'll do that." Wyn elbowed him out of the way. "Maybe you should call Doug, see if he's learned anything."

He nodded and glanced over to see Rocky standing near the front door, the dog's signal that he needed to go out. "I'll call after I take Rocky out."

"Okay." She took over the dishes.

He hadn't removed his boots from his earlier trip outside with Rocky to get his food and doggy dishes. He pulled on his coat, hat, and gloves, then opened the front door. Rocky trotted outside, lifted his nose to the air, and sniffed with interest.

The early morning dawn seemed encouraging. No snow in the forecast today, which he decided was a good thing. Not that anything, even a blizzard, would keep him from searching for Eli. The need to move through any type of weather was exactly why he'd brought the snow machines along in the first place.

He stood waiting patiently, knowing Rocky would get down to business without being told. Probably sooner if he didn't tell the dog to get busy. He swept his gaze around the area but didn't notice anything unusual. Two houses to the right, he could see there was a light on in Shana's house.

He was curious about the relationship the young teacher had with his son. He was glad the little boy enjoyed being in her preschool class, and it was obvious by the way Shana had brought Eli home with her that she gave him additional one-on-one attention during the time it took for Wynona to get home from work.

For a split second, he was jealous of the closeness Shana had with his son. A special bond, a relationship he didn't have. Might never have.

No, he refused to consider that option. He would forge a relationship with his son. Granted, it may take time. Weeks for sure. Maybe even months. Up to a year.

A depressing thought, but he quickly shoved it aside. He

didn't care how long it took. He would exude a patience that he'd never displayed before. As Rocky trotted off to finally get down to business, he wryly realized he and his partner were alike in one way.

Stubborn and independent.

After cleaning up after Rocky, he headed back to the front door. As usual, it took Rocky a full minute to decide whether to accompany him. He sighed and opened the door.

Rocky finally turned and trotted toward him.

As he shrugged out of his coat, his phone rang. Seeing Doug's name on the screen, he quickly answered. "Hey, Doug. What's going on?"

"I just heard from Griff. He and his team are en route to the scene of the fire. He would like to speak with you and Wynona about the case, and of course, he wants that shell casing you found."

"I have the shell casing in my pocket." Chase glanced at Wyn who was obviously listening. He should have put the call on speaker for her benefit. "Of course, Wynona and I would be glad to discuss the case with the FBI," he said. "We'll meet agent Griff Flannery at the trailer house."

"Great," Doug said. "I knew you would, so he's already expecting you to be there. I'm guessing he'll be there in about thirty to forty minutes."

"Thirty to forty minutes sounds good to me," he repeated for Wynona's sake. "What about your tech guy, Ian Dunlap? Have you spoken to him?"

"Yes, I've given him the name of your suspect, Julia Stone," Doug said. "Ian has agreed to get right to work on seeing what he could find about her." Doug paused, then added, "Keep in mind, Ian doesn't work for me anymore. He may have to abandon the search in favor of working more pressing cases back in Wisconsin."

"I know." He decided not to reiterate that for Wyn. She needed to stay positive. "I understand. Anything Ian can come up with would be very helpful."

"I called another tech friend of mine, a guy by the name of Gabe Melrose," Doug went on. "He works for the Milwaukee Police Department's tactical team. He's getting married to a cop by the name of Cassidy Sommer next week, but he agreed to see if he could find anything on Julia Stone too."

Chase was touched by Doug's efforts. "Thank you so much. Having two tech experts digging into Julia Stone is going above and beyond."

"Not really, and they haven't come up with anything yet," Doug said modestly. "But we're doing everything possible on our end."

"Thanks." He glanced down at Rocky who was rolling around on his back as if trying to scratch an itch. "If we find anything useful, I'll call. If we can identify an area to begin searching, I may need backup."

"Maya and Zion are ready to go at any time," Doug assured him. "Jessica and her K9 Teddy want to help too."

"They may get their chance." At least, he hoped so. Teddy was more of a drug-sniffing dog, but Jess had been cross-training him with other scents too. "Take care, Doug. Stay in touch."

"You too." Doug ended the call.

"The FBI wants to talk to us?" Wyn asked. "Does that mean they're taking over Eli's kidnapping case?"

"I'm not sure," he admitted. "I know the feds don't like to overstep, especially when jurisdiction rests with the tribal police. But Eli is a young child, so I'm hoping they do take over the investigation. I think we need all the resources we can get."

"I agree." A glimmer of hope shone in her brown eyes. "I want everyone out there looking for Eli."

He did too. But the rez was a large place, and other than the burned shell of the trailer house, they didn't know where to start. "Let's head out to the trailer home now. I know the feds won't be there for a while, but maybe we can look around. See if Rocky can come up with anything new."

"Yes! I'd like that." Wyn was almost back to her usual self, and his heart ached for what they'd lost. He took a step toward her, then caught himself. This wasn't the time to think about rekindling their relationship.

No matter how much he wanted to.

He'd never been interested in dating after Wyn. Sure, he could blame the airplane crash that had stolen his parents. Or the need to be there for his younger siblings. To spend every spare minute they had searching the mountainside area that was the most likely spot where their plane had gone down.

But he knew the real reason was that he still cared about her. And now that they'd been thrown together in the search for their son, he was glad he'd never found anyone else.

And that she hadn't either.

"I'm ready." Wyn's statement interrupted my thoughts. Her long hair had dried and was shiny in the pool of sunlight streaming in from the eastern window.

"Okay." He pulled himself back to the issue at hand. He belatedly realized she had the computer tucked under her arm and realized it would be smart to bring it along. Pulling on his coat, he glanced at Rocky. "Give me a minute to store his food and dishes in the back of the SUV." Better to be prepared for a long day than to be forced to buy dog food along the way. On the ranch, they used a rather expensive brand, mostly because their dogs were their livelihood and worth every penny. Of course, they'd had to make do with other brands in a pinch.

He hauled the bucket of kibble and the dishes out to the SUV. Then he took another few minutes to slide the vest back over Rocky's head, cinching it around his chest. Rock took the vest in stride because he loved the search game.

"Get up," he said, gesturing to the back crate area. For once, Rocky obliged without complaint.

Wyn was already settled in the passenger seat with the laptop. He opened his door and leaned in. "I'm going to connect the trailer too, okay?"

Her eyes widened. "You think we'll need it?"

"I'm not sure, but I'd rather be prepared." He stepped back, closed the door, and then set about removing the trailer lock and connecting the snowmobile trailer to the hitch on the SUV.

Five minutes later, he slid in behind the wheel and started the engine. His fingers were frozen, and he held them in front of the heating vents for a few seconds to warm them up. The sun may be on the rise, but the wind was still freezing cold. "Let's go."

The trip back to the trailer house didn't take long, but seeing the blackened ruins was like taking a fist to the gut. It looked bad.

Really bad.

He didn't see how it was possible anything left behind by the kidnappers would be processed as evidence. Yet he pushed forward, only pulling over to the side of the road when he reached the same spot they'd parked in last night.

Or early this morning. The timeline was foggy in his brain.

Wyn had her hands over her mouth, staring in horror at what was left behind. He reached out to touch her arm. "Don't worry. I'm sure the feds will salvage something out of this."

She lowered her hands and nodded. "Okay. What's next?"

"I'm going to send Rocky off to do a search." He hit the back hatch to let his K9 out. "From there, we'll move a few miles away and try to have him search again."

She didn't appear hopeful but pushed open her door. He quickly got out too and went around back for Rocky.

"Are you ready?" He poured water into a bowl as he spoke, revving the dog up. "Are you? Are you ready to search?" He set the bowl on the ground and reached for the bag containing Eli's clothing. Rocky surprised him by slurping a bit of the water. He opened the bag for the dog. Rocky sniffed for a moment, then lifted his nose to the air. "Search! Let's search for Eli!"

With his nose still held high, Rocky trotted in the general direction of the burned rubble of the trailer house. As he had earlier, he began to take a zigzag pattern moving in the direction of the driveway and the general location where the front door had been.

Rocky sat at the spot and let out a sharp bark.

"Good boy," he praised the K9's alert. "Search! Search for Eli!"

The scent of smoke had obliterated whatever scents Eli had left inside the house, so he wasn't surprised when the dog wheeled away from the wreckage in another zigzag pattern. He hurried to keep up with Rocky just in case the dog was able to pick up a scent trail.

Wyn hurried to join them. Neither of them spoke for a few long minutes. The dog was headed west, and it took him a minute to realize the wind was coming from that direction, blowing from west to east.

Suddenly Rocky stopped and lifted his snout to the air. Then he took off like a rocket.

"What caught his attention?" Wyn asked.

"I don't know. But hopefully, we'll find out." Rocky wasn't prone to false alerts. He didn't get distracted often. Chase's heart lodged in his throat as he broke into a run to keep up with his K9.

Maybe, just maybe, Rocky had caught Eli's scent.

8

Following Chase and Rocky, Wyn's heart swelled with hope. After seeing the K9 in action, she felt certain the dog had caught Eli's scent. She wished they'd have spread out last night to continue searching. Then again, it wouldn't have been easy to navigate through the area in the darkness.

Rocky abruptly slowed his pace, sniffing the air, then backtracking as if he'd lost track of the scent. Her excitement plummeted to the soles of her feet. She caught up to Chase, breathing heavily. "What do you think? Did he find, then lose Eli's scent?"

"I'm not sure," he admitted, glancing around. There were houses in this area that appeared nicer than the trailer park they'd left behind. "The wind is coming from the west. Could be that he caught a whiff of Eli's scent from some-place the boy had been taken. Rocky doesn't often make mistakes or provide false alerts." They slowed to a walk as Rocky continued to stand sniffing the air. "I'm not sure what to do. We may have to turn back around to get the SUV. We could drive a mile or so, then have Rocky try again."

She tried not to show her stark disappointment. She'd hoped the dog would lead them straight to her son. But she should have known it wouldn't be that easy.

Nothing about this nightmare had been simple or straightforward. She didn't even understand why Eli had been taken.

"Whatever you think is best." She glanced at Chase. "I don't want to give up the search, though."

"We won't." Chase frowned. "Although it seems a little strange that Rocky would have caught his sent like this."

Her heart squeezed in her chest. "Why? Because you think they have Eli outside?"

Chase grimaced. "I'm not sure what's going on."

She couldn't bear the idea of the kidnappers keeping Eli outside in the freezing cold temperatures. No way would a child last long outside in wintertime. A sudden thought occurred to her. "Eli had a runny nose." She reached out to grab Chase's arm. "I'm not sure how a human's scent works, but he could have swiped his face on his coat sleeve and then brushed up against the truck." She frowned. "Could Rocky be alerting to Eli's scent clinging to the outside of the white truck?"

"That's possible." Chase glanced around at their current location. "And if that is the case, that Rocky is tracking the scent shedding off the truck, then we for sure need to turn back to get the SUV."

It was a disappointing end to a promising trail. She swallowed hard and nodded. "Okay, that works. I pray Rocky will be able to pick up the scent again."

"Me too," Chase said grimly. They turned to retrace their steps back to the burned trailer. With the wind at their backs now, they made decent progress without needing to break into a run while wearing their winter gear.

When they reached the site of the fire, she noticed another SUV coming down the road toward what was left of the building. Glancing at her watch, she was surprised to see that a good forty minutes had passed. "Is that the FBI agent?"

"Yeah. See the white box truck lagging behind?" Chase gestured toward it with his gloved hand. "I'm sure that belongs to the crime scene techs."

She continued walking toward his SUV before realizing he hadn't kept up with her. A flash of annoyance hit hard. She wanted to get in the SUV to continue their search for Eli, not stand here chatting with the feds.

But they had promised to be interviewed. She lifted her head to the sky seeking strength.

"We'll be back on the road soon," Chase promised, reading her expression. "I'm sure this won't take long."

She wasn't convinced about that. Yet what could she say? Rocky had lost the scent, and there was no guarantee that he'd alert again. Swallowing her protest, she turned away from the SUV to join him.

The black SUV rolled to a stop. A tall, lean man with dark hair emerged from behind the wheel. He held up his badge and ID, then quickly stuffed it back into his pocket. "You must be Chase Sullivan and Wynona Blackhorse."

"Yes. Thanks for coming." Chase gave him a nod.

Special Agent in Charge Griff Flannery was younger than she'd expected. Maybe her age of thirty-two or slightly younger. He didn't come across as arrogant, though, which she took as a good sign.

After taking down their full names and phone numbers, the federal agent got down to business. "You can call me Griff; we don't use formal titles around here. Would you mind starting at the beginning? I've been given part of the story from Doug, but I'd rather hear directly from the source. I feel a little like I've been dropped into the middle of a movie without understanding who the characters are or what's happening."

"My four-and-a-half-year-old son Elijah was taken from his preschool teacher's home yesterday afternoon, sometime between four and five o'clock," she said. "His teacher, Shana Wildbloom, was assaulted. I found her lying on the floor with a wound on the side of her temple with no sign of Eli. She mentioned a man wearing a ski mask came inside and struck her. After making sure Eli wasn't hiding in the house, I called Chase. I also called the tribal police." She hesitated, then pushed on without mentioning the blood relationship between Chase and her son. "The Sullivan K9 Search and Rescue Ranch is well known throughout the state, and I wanted his family's expertise to find my son."

"I asked my K9, Rocky, to search on Eli's scent." Chase picked up the story. "He alerted in Shana's house, of course, but he also alerted near the side of the road several yards down from the scene of the crime. Shana noticed a white pickup truck parked there, but it was gone by then. From there, we spread out to continue the search. Rocky ultimately alerted here, at the trailer home."

Everyone took a somber moment to eye the burned building.

"I should have stayed to watch over the evidence," Chase said. "I take full responsibility for the lapse in judgment."

Agent Flannery waved that away. "You couldn't have known they'd come back to torch the place."

Chase shrugged, but she knew he still blamed himself. "Anyway, Rocky alerted outside the front door at first, which gave us hope that Eli had been there. The door wasn't locked, so we went inside. Rock alerted again in the living room near the sofa. Unfortunately, the place was empty, and it looked to me as if they may have left in a hurry."

"What makes you say that?" Flannery asked.

"Because they left two half-filled bottles of beer behind on the kitchen table. I'm sure they belonged to the kidnappers. Until then, we didn't know how many people were involved." Chase shrugged. "Now we have reason to believe there are two of them. And there could be others. For all we know, these guys have been hired by someone else to do the job."

"Yeah, Doug mentioned the beer bottles as potential evidence," Flannery said. "And the shell casing, which you need to give me. As far as the beer bottles go, the fire wouldn't burn hot enough to melt the glass. If we're able to find them, we have the potential to test for DNA."

"How long will that take?" Wyn tried not to sound impatient. "Eli's been gone for more fifteen hours already. We need to find him today. Before it gets dark again."

"I'll put a rush on them," Flannery promised. "But I can't lie. It's likely going to take a couple of days."

She turned away, biting her lip to keep herself from lashing out at him. They needed to find Eli in the next few hours, not days.

She was already losing hope that the kidnappers would call with a ransom demand. The hour was going on eight o'clock. If they wanted her to go to the bank to get money, they'd have told her by now.

But they hadn't. Which meant they wanted something other than money.

Chase handed over the shell casing Rocky had found, then crossed over to put his arm around her shoulders. Rocky came, too, bumping her with his nose. The dog made her want to smile, but her face felt frozen. As if her skin would crack if she tried to smile. Chase squeezed her gently. "Hey, don't worry. We're not giving up. We'll keep doing our part."

She gave a jerky nod. "I know. It's just . . ."

"We'll find him," Chase said firmly. "I have faith in God and Rocky's nose."

"Can we leave now, then?" She turned to see Agent Flannery greeting the crime scene techs who'd emerged from the boxy white van. Rocky didn't seem interested in meeting the newcomers. Despite his independence, she noticed the dog stood in a protective stance between them. He didn't growl or bark, but she sensed he would if anyone made a move toward them. She almost wished she'd gotten Eli a dog. One that would have protected him from the ski-masked intruder.

"Just give me a few minutes." Chase glanced thoughtfully at the burned house. "I'd like to know if the bottles are even in there. No point in waiting to hear on testing if there's no evidence to process."

That was true. She followed him to the charred opening where the front door had been. Rocky trotted with them. He didn't alert this time, and she wondered if he was smart enough to know he'd already done that.

And that they wanted him to alert on new locations.

They stood back watching as the crime scene techs donned their white Tyvek protective gear, then gingerly made their way inside. Agent Flannery went in, too, being careful not to touch anything. The scent of charred wood and smoke was incredibly strong, and she couldn't help but wonder if the burning smell would interfere with Rocky's ability to scent Eli.

After a moment, someone yelled out. "I found a beer bottle!"

"Two of them," the other said with satisfaction. "We've got two bottles here in what looks to be the kitchen."

"Good work," Griff Flannery praised. "Let's get those items into evidence bags." The agent turned back to face them. "Like I said, I'll see if the lab can turn the results around as soon as possible. Same with the shell casing."

"Thank you." She appreciated his efforts, even if she suspected they would be too late. She glanced expectantly at Chase.

"We're going to expand our search zone," Chase explained to Flannery. "Rocky seemed to catch a whiff of Eli's scent, but then lost it. With the wind coming in from the west, we're going to drive that way for a few miles and try again."

Griff looked at the dog. "I'd love to see him in action. But I'll need to stay here until we've processed the scene. Call me if he alerts on anything specific."

"We will," she said quickly, reassured that the feds were taking an active role in the case.

"Take my card." Flannery pulled it from his coat pocket. "I have your contact information, too, so we can keep in touch."

"Thanks." Chase tucked the card away. "That reminds me, the trailer house is owned by Julia Stone. Wynona found her on the tribal housing registry, but there's no contact information, and we haven't been able to find anything else that she owns. Doug has his tech buddy working on finding out more about her."

"I'll follow up with Doug soon," Flannery promised. "It'll be interesting if she even realizes her property has been destroyed by a fire."

"Agree," Chase said. It was all Wyn could do not to grab

Chase's arm to yank him away. She wanted to get back out on the road to find Eli.

Griff Flannery gave them a nod. "Keep in touch." He turned back toward what was left of the trailer house. Chase finally headed toward the SUV.

Five minutes later, they were back on the road. But Wyn still couldn't relax. They couldn't wait for the DNA. That would take too long.

No, they needed more. She prayed with all her heart that Rocky would alert again on Eli's scent.

TENSION RADIATED off Wynona in tangible waves. Even Rocky seemed to notice, his face pressed against the screen of his crate.

Telling her to relax would be useless, so Chase focused on picturing the map of this portion of the city in his mind. There were open fields to the north, but he vaguely remembered there was another residential area not too far away.

Eyeing the odometer, he figured they'd go two miles before trying Rocky's nose again. He wasn't sure this plan of his would work, but he couldn't come up with anything better. He considered calling Doug for an update, then realized he was being ridiculous. If his tech experts had found something, Doug would let him know.

"Is this far enough?" Wyn asked.

He glanced at the odometer. "Another half mile, then I'll pull over."

She twisted in her seat to look at Rocky. "I really hope he alerts on Eli's scent. If he's somehow following the truck, it could be miles from here by now."

He understood her frustration. He was about to remind

her that the only reason they'd turned around to head back to the trailer in the first place was because Rocky had lost the scent trail. But he held his tongue, knowing that pointing out the obvious wouldn't help her feel any better.

In truth, he wasn't happy about the delay either. He'd hoped the kidnappers wouldn't take their son too far. They could have come this way last night but hadn't. At the time, he'd blamed the darkness.

Now he was second-guessing himself all over again.

A moment later, he spotted an open area between two houses that looked like a good place to pull over. He parked along the side of the road, making sure the trailer cleared the driveway behind them.

"This looks like a good place to resume our search." Wyn was clearly trying to stay positive.

He managed a smile. "I hope so." He hit the latch to release Rocky from the back. "Let's go to work."

Thankfully, Rocky was always eager to play the search game. He offered the scent bag, but Rocky gave him what seemed to be an exasperated look, as if to say, *Yeah, I got it.*

"Are you ready to go?" His K9 didn't need much encouragement. "Search! Search for Eli!"

Just like earlier, Rocky lifted his nose to the air and sniffed for a long moment. Chase checked the area, confirming the wind was still coming across a western direction. The jagged peaks of the Teton mountain range pierced the sky.

Rocky quickly began to trot in his zigzag pattern, sniffing along the ground at times, then lifting his nose to the air. The dog didn't take off like a rocket the way he had earlier, but meandered along as if determined to pick up the scent.

Wyn kept pace beside him. The way she kept glancing over at him made him think she wanted to say something.

"What is it?" he finally asked.

"It doesn't look to me like he's following a specific scent," she said, nodding at the Elkhound. "How long do we let him search like this before calling a halt and moving on another few miles?"

He gestured toward his K9. "It's best to let Rocky take the lead. I don't think we should give up too soon. If he gets tired, he'll let me know. That would be a good time to stop for a break anyway."

"Oh, okay." She looked disappointed.

They kept going for almost a full mile before Rocky abruptly lifted his head and quickened his pace. His K9's response caused a jolt of adrenaline to surge through him. He sprinted after his dog, hoping Wyn would keep up.

She did.

Rocky continued following the invisible path before him. At one point, the dog turned to go around a house, then continued cutting through another person's yard. Being winter, there weren't people working outside to object to their presence. Still, he wondered if one of them would put a call in to the tribal police. Or worse, come after them with a gun.

Rocky made another abrupt turn, heading south. For a moment, Chase worried his dog had gotten distracted again. He was about to call him back to refresh his focus on the scent when Rocky made another turn to head west.

Beside him, Wyn's breath became loud and labored. She was in good shape, but they weren't exactly dressed for outdoor running. Breathing in the cold air felt like inhaling razors into his lungs.

"Do you want me to take a break?" he asked.

"No! Keep—going." Her voice hitched. "If I can't—make it, keep—going!"

He found himself slowing his pace so as not to leave her behind. "We're in this together, Wyn."

"Just—find—Eli!"

He figured it was okay to fall behind a bit, as long as Rocky was within sight. But when Rocky disappeared behind a hill, he had little choice but to do as she asked. Putting on a burst of speed, he closed the gap.

He was getting tired now, too, but pushed himself to keep going. While his K9 hadn't alerted at all, Rocky still seemed to be anxious to get to a specific location.

After cresting the hill, he frowned. Where had Rocky gone? He kept moving west, hoping that was the correct direction. Two minutes later, he spotted the Elkhound near the corner of a house.

He caught up to Rocky who didn't alert. The dog moved back and forth across the snow-covered ground, then stopped and lifted his nose to the air. His heart sank, and he hoped the K9 hadn't lost the scent again.

Glancing back over his shoulder, Chase could see Wyn was cresting the hill. She hadn't fallen too far behind. Deciding his dog needed a break, he called, "Heel. Rocky, heel!"

Rocky ignored him for a long moment, then trotted back to his side. The dog stared up at him, as if saying he wanted to keep going. Looking down at his smartwatch, Chase could see they'd gone almost two miles.

Maybe he should have driven farther down the road before letting Rocky out to find the trail. If they pressed forward, it would take that much longer to get back to the SUV.

"Keep going," Wyn called, her voice stronger now.

He shook his head. "No. We need to return to the SUV." At her crestfallen expression, he added, "Wyn, we've covered two miles. It's going to take us thirty minutes or more to get back."

"Maybe we should have used the snow machines." She sighed, then bent at the waist, bracing her hands on her thighs, taking long deep breaths. "I can't believe we've followed Rocky for two miles."

He nodded, willing his pulse to settle. "That's how it is sometimes. The dog doesn't get as tired as we do." He shrugged. "Maybe we should use the snowmobiles. Either way, it's time to head back."

Before they could turn around, Rocky lifted his head and broke into another run. He was tempted to call the dog back when the K9 veered around a clump of bushes.

Muttering under his breath, he glanced at Wyn. "Stay here for a minute. I'll see what caught his attention."

"Nope." Her cheeks were flushed. "I'm sticking close."

He broke into a slow jog, following Rocky's path. Again, when he rounded the cluster of brush, there was no sign of the dog.

"Where is he?" Wyn asked.

"Who knows? That dog has a mind of his own." He slowed to a stop, listening intently. When he didn't hear an alert, he continued walking. "Don't worry, Rock will eventually come back to find us."

"He has way more energy than I do," she grumbled. "I can't believe your entire family does search and rescue missions like this."

"Can't lie, it's much easier in the warmer weather, that's for sure." He frowned and scanned the ground for Rocky's tracks. "This way." He turned to head north.

"I really hope this isn't some sort of wild-goose chase," Wyn said wearily.

He couldn't deny he was getting concerned about that

possibility as well. Rocky's behavior this morning wasn't that unusual. The K9 could be extremely stubborn when he was on the hunt. Yet Chase was also keenly aware that his dog hadn't alerted on a specific location. He prayed Rocky wasn't on the wrong path.

They cut through another yard, then followed the dog's tracks to the north. He had his compass but still felt a bit turned around. Good thing his SUV could be located via his phone.

They walked in silence for another five minutes without seeing any sign of Rocky. Chase was getting more annoyed by the minute. Where was the K9?

Then he heard a sharp bark.

Wyn's hand grabbed his arm. "Is that an alert?"

"Maybe. Let's hurry." He pushed himself back into a run, following Rocky's faint tracks in the hard-packed snow. They turned south again, then rounded another cluster of trees.

Beyond that was a house. The sun wasn't high in the sky, but the reflection bounced off the snow, making it hard to see.

"There!" Wyn cried out, pointing to their left. They had almost gone too far. "He's over by the driveway!"

Not the front door? Chase wondered why the scent would be stronger there along the driveway rather than at the entrance to the residence. Yet there was no denying Rocky was sitting and staring at him intently.

He hurried forward. "What is it, Rocky? What did you find?"

Rocky remained still as a statue, giving him that intense stare as if Chase should figure out what was going on in the dog's mind. He stopped next to his K9 and examined the ground.

There were at least two sets of footprints in the snow. And there were tire tracks as well. He wasn't an expert, but they appeared to be the same make and model as the ones they'd discovered outside the trailer house.

"Here?" Wyn asked hoarsely. "Eli was here?"

"I think so." He was about to tell Rocky to search again, thinking this wasn't the only spot that Eli had been, when he caught a glimpse of something in the ground. He hadn't noticed it earlier because Rocky was practically sitting on top of it.

"Rocky, heel."

For once, Rocky didn't ignore him. The dog rose to his four feet and backed away from the alert location. His K9 didn't go as far as to come sit at his side in the heel position, but Chase quickly decided to let that lapse go. He and the dog could fight over the position of being the alpha later.

He took two steps forward, then slowly lowered to a crouch.

Now he could see the item buried in the snow more clearly. It was a small square building block.

His breath caught in his throat. It was an exact match to those scattered across the floor at Shana's house.

9

Rocky had found one of Eli's blocks!

Wyn spun to stare at the house that was only a few feet away. It was nicer than the trailer house. "Was Eli inside there too?"

"Not sure, but we're not taking any chances." Chase grabbed her arm. "We'll call Griff and ask him to head out here."

As much as she wanted to rush inside the house, she knew Chase was right to be cautious. The home was nicer than the previous trailer house, but it was dark inside, and there were no vehicles in the driveway. It wasn't likely that Eli was inside.

"Hurry," she urged.

Chase already has his phone out. "Griff? Rocky alerted on Eli's scent, and we found one of his toy building blocks in the snow outside a single-story residence." She stopped listening as he explained their current location. "Great. See you soon."

"Will you at least ask Rocky to search for Eli?" she asked.

"We know Eli was here; he dropped his block," Chase

said gently. "Rocky alerting at the front door doesn't tell us anything new."

"How can you be so logical?" She threw up her hands in frustration. "Our son was here, Chase. He was here!"

"I know that." Chase's voice was low and husky. "Do you think I don't want to charge inside too? I do. More than anything. But we're going to wait the few minutes it will take for the FBI to get here."

His calm attitude was driving her crazy. Yet she was so glad they hadn't stopped the search to head back to the SUV. What if the wind had shifted again and Rocky hadn't found and alerted on Eli's scent?

She stared down at the wooden block partially hidden in the snow. While she was thrilled to see it, she knew her son would be upset at losing it. "I hope Eli still has his stuffed horsey."

"Me too." Chase turned to glance down the street from the direction they'd come. "See? That didn't take long."

She turned in time to see a black SUV approaching. She was surprised. It seemed as if Griff Flannery had jumped into the car to head over the moment Chase called.

While Chase walked over to greet the FBI agent, she stayed where she was, standing over the building block. The block was for the letter C, and it was the only tangible lead to Eli. The way Rocky had found it only reinforced her belief that Chase and Rocky offered the best chance of rescuing the little boy.

She listened as Chase filled Griff Flannery on the sequence of events that had led Rocky to alerting on the block. The FBI agent crossed over and bent to examine it. Then he looked up at her. "You're sure this is Eli's?"

"Yes. He was playing with the blocks when he was

taken." She frowned. "To be honest, I didn't look closely enough to notice that one of them was missing."

Griff nodded and pulled an evidence bag from his pocket. After using the plastic like a glove and picking up the block, he rose. "Okay, I need you and Chase to stay behind me. I'll take the lead. Once I've cleared the place, you can bring Rocky inside to search for Eli's scent."

She chafed at the delay but didn't argue. At least this time, the house wouldn't go up in a ball of flames.

"FBI!" Griffin pounded on the front door. "Open up! FBI!"

There was no answer from inside.

Griff tried again, then reached for the front door. It swung open easily, meaning it wasn't locked.

Eli wasn't there. At least, not anymore.

She hadn't really expected him to be, but it still hurt to have come so close to finding him, only to fail. She swallowed hard and waited for Griff to clear the house. It didn't take long for him to reappear in the doorway.

"I'm going to have the crime scene techs head over here to process the interior of the home." Griff gestured to the dog. "If you want to use Rocky to verify that Eli was here, that's fine. Don't touch anything, and when that's finished, I need you both to stay outside."

"Understood." Chase glanced at her, then turned his attention to Rocky. "Are you ready to search? Are you? Search!" Chase opened the front door. Griff stood off to the side to stay out of the way. "Search for Eli!"

Rocky didn't need much encouragement. The K9 trotted up to the front door and crossed the threshold. She hurried over to watch. Just like at the trailer house, the dog went to the sofa, sniffed intently, then sat and let out a sharp bark.

"Good boy," Chase praised.

"Impressive," Griff said. "Do you want to do the rest of the house?"

Chase glanced at her briefly, then shook his head. "No need. We have the block outside and the alert. Eli was here. And he's not anymore. We need to know who owns this place and where the kidnappers have taken Eli from here."

The last part of his statement was sobering. Wyn knew she could find the owner of the house using the tribal housing database. But finding where Eli was now wouldn't be easy.

"I don't suppose the kidnappers left anything else behind?" She held Griff's gaze. "Like a piece of paper, a note, a phone . . ."

"Nothing that I can see," Griff said. "But I promise to let you know if the crime scene techs come up with something that will help. If we're able to get fingerprints, those can be processed and sent through the system very quickly." The agent shrugged. "If our perps are in the system, we'll have results very soon."

That was encouraging. "Thank you." She backed away from the house so Chase and Rocky could join her.

Chase took a moment to reward the K9 with the red ball. Rocky dropped into a playful pose, then took off running with the ball in his mouth. He was like a kid with a new toy, and she was a little surprised at how well the reward of playing ball seemed to be received. Under different circumstances, she'd have asked about his training.

But now she was ready to move on to the next phase of the investigation.

Inside, she could see Griff was already on the phone with his team. She shivered in the cold. "I guess we walk back to the SUV and trailer?"

"Yes. But let's hurry," Chase said. "You were smart

enough to bring the laptop. We can use my phone as a hotspot so you can log in to get the name of the property owner."

She nodded. "I like that plan."

They alternated between walking and jogging back to where they'd left the SUV. Chase had used an app on his phone to locate the vehicle since they'd crossed many yards in following Rocky's trail. The dog ran, too, seeming to enjoy the outing. Chase let Rocky keep the red ball longer than usual, and it was only once they'd finally reached the SUV that he told the dog to hand him the ball.

Rocky dropped the ball at her feet.

"You're a brat, Rock." Chase bent down to pick up the ball. "A real brat."

Rocky wagged his tail in agreement.

Chase opened the rear hatch for the K9. Rocky jumped inside, then stretched out with his head down between his paws. She slid into the passenger seat and picked up the computer that was ice cold to the touch. She hoped the battery would work in the frigid temps.

Chase started the car engine. She held the laptop near the heating vents, waiting for the air to turn warm. After a long minute, she opened the laptop and powered it up.

It worked. She glanced over at Chase who was fiddling with his phone. After a moment, she saw a message appear in the upper right-hand corner of the computer asking if she wanted to connect to the hotspot. She clicked the link, waited another few seconds, then brought up the Wind River tribal property registry.

It took her a while to identify the proper residence. There were addresses associated with homes, but many of them were not posted outside for mail delivery. Out here, most people used post office boxes rather than having their mail delivered to their homes. That practice had changed a bit here in Riverton, but the home where the building block had been found didn't have an address posted in clear view.

"I found it!" She toggled from the map to the registry, double-checking her work. "The house is owned by Carl Longfoot." She did a quick search to see if Carl Longfoot owned any other properties in the area.

He didn't.

"Does that name sound familiar to you?" Chase asked.

"No." She desperately wished it did. She knew the tribal leaders, of course, but none of them were named Longfoot. Or Stone.

"Keep looking," Chase encouraged.

"I am. This is so strange," Wyn said, half to herself as she worked the keyboard. "I'm in the tribal registry, and just like Julia Stone, there's only one person with the last name of Longfoot." She shook her head in frustration. "I don't get it. Most of the people living here have families. Large and extended families. It's highly unusual that the two people owning properties used by these kidnappers seem to be single individuals without any sort of extended family."

"Without an extended family with the same last name." Chase clarified her statement. "As we said before, both Julia Stone and Carl Longfoot could have family members on the reservation under a different name. We don't know for sure they haven't remarried, divorced, or changed their name for some other reason."

"Maybe." She was frustrated with the lack of information. "But I'd really expected to find some sort of connection between them."

"I would have thought so too." Chase pulled away from the side of the road, driving toward the property that Griff was having processed by the crime scene techs. "Let's head over to let Griff know this guy's name."

"Sure." She tried to come up with another way to find relatives of either of the homeowners. "There must be some connection between Julia Stone and Carl Longfoot," she repeated. "If we can find that connection, then we may know who's responsible for taking Eli."

Chase nodded. "I agree, but who would know that?"

She stared at the screen for a moment. "My father. Or really, any of the tribal leaders may recognize their names. I should call him anyway." She swallowed a wave of guilt. "I never told my father Eli had been taken."

"No way. I don't like that idea." Chase's tone was sharp. "We still don't know for sure that this isn't related to your audit work. Maybe one of the tribal leaders is behind the kidnapping to keep you from digging into the audit."

"I don't think that's the reason," she objected wearily. "And speaking of my job, I never called in to say I was taking the day off." She was a little surprised no one had reached out to her. "I should do that now."

"Wait." Chase grabbed her arm. "Isn't there another way? Someone else you can talk to about these homeowners?"

She shook her head. "I'm sorry, but I don't know anyone who can provide that information." She thought about it for a moment, then said, "Although now that we're talking about it, I think it would be better if the request for information didn't come from you or me, but from the FBI."

"Yeah, I like that approach." Chase looked relieved. "Go ahead and call off sick. But don't say anything about Eli."

"Okay." As she prepared to make the call to her assistant, Evelyn, she couldn't help wondering if keeping Eli's kidnapping a secret was the right thing to do. When she'd first realized he was missing, she'd wanted every single person on the rez to be out looking for her son.

Now she didn't know what to think. So far, their evidence indicated Eli had been kept here in Riverton at least for the past several hours.

She hadn't taken Chase's suggestion about her audit of the tribal council funds being a reason for the kidnapping seriously. Yet the fact that Eli had been moved around the city, and a fire had been used to destroy evidence—not to mention being shot at—gave her pause.

Was Chase right? Was it possible that someone within the tribal council was responsible for kidnapping their son?

And if so, what would he demand in exchange for bringing him home?

CHASE NOTICED the crime scene tech's white panel van was in the driveway when he approached the house that they now knew belonged to a man by the name of Carl Longfoot. Nobody was outside, though, so he assumed they were already hard at work lifting fingerprints from inside.

He would have rather found Eli inside, but having a relatively fresh crime scene to examine and process for clues was better than what they'd had before.

"Stay here while I update Griff." Chase pulled off to the side of the road and parked. "This won't take long."

"Okay." She was scowling at her computer. "I'll keep trying to figure out if there's any other way I can dig into the backgrounds of these homeowners."

Leaving her to it, and keeping the car engine running, he pushed out of the driver's side and headed up to the house. Griff looked surprised to see him.

"Back so soon?"

"The homeowner is Carl Longfoot." Chase got straight to the point. "Much like with Julia Stone, Wynona hasn't been able to find any of Carl's extended family." He could see the crime scene techs were dusting for prints. "Have you found anything?"

"Several prints, but it's going to take time to isolate and run them through the system," Griff said. "We're working as quickly as we can." Griff gestured to the activity going on inside. "They have a computer set up inside the white van, so we should know something within the hour. If they're in the system," Griff added. "You know there is a slim possibility they're not former criminals."

"I know." He was hoping that these two men who had taken Eli did have criminal backgrounds. But he also knew that prints didn't always go into the system for petty crimes. "Do you mind if I call Doug? Maybe his tech guy can find something on Carl Longfoot."

"Go ahead, we'll take whatever leads Doug's guys can find." Griff didn't seem to have the typical arrogance of a federal agent. Not that he was an expert, but Maya had mentioned her previous interactions with the FBI in her law enforcement days. But then the agent in charge retired, and he assumed Griff was the new kid on the block.

"Great. Thanks again." Chase didn't want to leave. He wanted to stand there to wait for the fingerprint results. But it was cold, and he knew that the process took time. With reluctance, he turned away.

He was halfway to the SUV when he heard the front door shut. Glancing over his shoulder, he saw a person dressed in Tyvek head toward the white panel van. His heart thumped crazily in his chest. He found himself taking several steps toward the van.

Then Griff came outside. "Chase, I told you I'll let you know what we find." The agent sounded irritable. Chase wanted to snap at him, then belatedly realized the fed didn't have any clue that the child they were looking for was his son.

"I know. I just thought I'd wait around a bit." He gestured toward the SUV. "Wyn is sick with fear. Eli is only four and a half, too young to be gone from his mother for this length of time."

"Yeah, yeah." Griff narrowed his gaze. "Weren't you involved in a missing kid here on the rez several months ago?"

The knot in his stomach tightened painfully. It was a case that haunted him from the moment Wyn had called him. "Yeah, the little girl's name was Alecia. Alecia Redstone." The image of the girl's dead body flashed in his mind. "She didn't make it."

Griff winced. "Sorry about that. But I heard you and your K9 did a great job in tracking her across the rez."

Not good enough, Chase thought darkly. "Rocky found her at the bottom of a ravine. We never knew if she fell of her own accord, was pushed, or was dumped."

There was a long moment of silence as the reality of what they were dealing with hit home for both men. "Wait here," Griff finally said. "I'll see what we've got."

Chase nodded without saying anything more. Dredging up the old wounds from his unsuccessful search for Alecia made him fear the same thing would happen here.

That he and Rocky would be too late to save Eli.

The sound of a car door slamming caused him to glance over to the SUV. Wyn had gotten out of the car and was hurrying toward him. "What is it?" she asked, deep furrows grooved into her brow. "Bad news?"

"No." He realized she'd picked up on his depressing thoughts. He jerked his thumb toward the panel van. "Good news actually. They're running the fingerprints they lifted from the kitchen now."

Her dark eyes widened. "Already? That's wonderful!"

"Yeah." He didn't want her to get her hopes up, but he knew it was too late. For him too. They desperately needed something to go on.

The next two minutes dragged by with excruciating slowness. He was about to head over to open the back of the panel van to find out what was happening when Griff emerged. The excitement in the FBI agent's expression made his heart race.

"You have something?" Chase asked.

Griff nodded and turned to look at Wyn. "Does the name George Twofeathers mean anything to you?"

"I don't think so." She frowned, then glanced at the SUV. "I can see if he has family listed in the tribal registry, though."

Wyn spun on her heel and ran to the SUV. Chase eyed Griff. "What crime did George Twofeathers commit? Why are his prints in the system?"

Griff hesitated, then said, "Armed robbery five years ago. He did his time and was released on good behavior. He's twenty-five years old now."

Chase wanted to punch something at the way this kid had been let back out on the streets to commit another crime. "If he's kidnapping kids, he's not behaving very well, is he?"

"Hey, it's not like releasing him was my decision," Griff protested. "That was up to the judge. And in all fairness, we don't know for sure he's involved."

"Then why are his prints in the house?" Chase knew his

anger was misplaced and did his best to wrestle it back. "I'm glad we have a name. You'll get a BOLO out for this guy? Do the tribal police know him?"

"I'll call them now." Griff pulled his phone from his pocket. He must have looked impatient because Griff sighed loudly. "Give me a break, Chase. I just got the fingerprint results. You stood here while we processed them. Now that we have a name to work from, we'll find him. I'm confident someone living on the rez will know him. Know his friends and where he hangs out. And before you ask, I checked to see if he has a car registered to his name. He doesn't."

That figured. Chase tried to think of another avenue to pursue. "Did you look at his arrest record? Did he have help pulling off the armed robbery?"

"Yes, but that guy's prints aren't in the house," Griff said. "He's a white guy by the name of Barry Tomlin. From what I saw, Tomlin is still in jail. Maybe he committed another crime while in lockup, and they added to his initial sentence."

He forced himself to nod. Griff was doing everything he could. Time for Chase to accept what they knew and to move on from there. "Okay, thanks. I really do appreciate everything you've done so far. Please keep me updated on your progress."

"Yeah, I will." Griff turned away to use his phone to call the tribal police.

Chase left him to it, heading back toward the SUV just as Wyn emerged from the passenger seat with a crestfallen expression etched on her face.

He swallowed a groan. "Let me guess. No home address for George Twofeathers?"

"Nope. I found his mother, Regina Twofeathers, but

she's not a property owner either." She gripped his arm. "We need to find her."

"I know." He reached over to put his arm around her shoulders. "We're getting close, Wyn. I can feel it."

"I hope you're right." She rested against him for a moment.

He held her close, ignoring the cold wind coming from the west. He wanted to kiss her, to let her know he still cared about her.

But before he could say anything, she pulled away. "I have an idea. I think we should check the apartments not far from the college."

He frowned. "Why there?"

"There are college kids living in those apartments. One or two of them could know George Twofeathers. I don't think he attended college, but kids of a certain age tend to hang out together, right?"

He nodded.

"I learned his mother, Regina, isn't very old, roughly forty-five years old. I'm assuming he might be about twenty-five give or take a year."

"He is twenty-five," he agreed. "Griff has his arrest record. George Twofeathers was arrested for armed robbery and spent five years in jail. That's why his prints are in the system."

"Has Griff issued an arrest warrant?"

"He's on the phone with the tribal police right now. I'm sure they'll head over to his last-known address, too, although if he has Eli, I doubt he's hanging around at his home." Chase glanced at the time. It was still pretty early, just going on nine in the morning. It seemed like an entire day had passed since they'd woken up this morning, rather than a few hours. "We can try the Silver Spur later, too, after the place opens. Maybe someone there knows him. Or who he hangs out with."

"You'll go with me?" Her expression was hopeful. "I can't sit here doing nothing, waiting for the feds and the tribal police to find George. If we can find a friend of his, maybe that's where they're holding Eli."

"Of course." He gave her another quick hug. "We're in this together."

"Thank you." Her voice was low and husky, and she surprised him by moving in to kiss him on the cheek. "I couldn't do any of this without you."

He stared down at her for a long moment. "Wyn, when this is over and we have Eli back," he began.

"I know," she quickly interrupted. "I know what you're going to say. That we need to talk about where we'll go from here. And we will. I—let's just wait to hash through the details of how we'll make things work until we find him."

He wanted to push for more but didn't. Maybe it was premature to plan their son's future when they didn't know where he was being held. Or why.

For now, they were a team, working toward the same goal.

To find their son.

10

As they returned to the SUV where Rocky waited patiently in the back, Wynona's thoughts whirled. She could only handle so much, and fear and panic over her missing son sat front and center in her mind.

Yet deep down, she knew Chase expected to, at the very least, share custody of their son. Would he go as far as to sue for sole custody? A shiver that had nothing to do with the cold ran down her spine. She didn't think so. And even if he tried, the courts would likely take Eli's diagnosis into consideration. Her son didn't know Chase. And yes, that was her fault. But it didn't change the facts.

She did her best to stay focused on their next steps. They had the name of a suspect, George Twofeathers. And while she hoped the tribal police would find him, that didn't mean she would sit back and wait for that to happen.

Chase pulled away from the house where they now knew Eli had been recently held. She wanted to believe that the plan wasn't to harm her son. But since she wasn't even sure why he'd been taken, she couldn't find much comfort in that thought.

"What do you think?" Chase glanced at her. "The apartments?"

"Actually, let's try the college first. That may be easier. Then we'll check the Silver Spur." Other than the two beer bottles that had been on the table in the trailer home, they didn't have any reason to believe George or his accomplice frequented the place.

"Sounds good to me," Chase agreed. He turned the SUV and trailer at the next intersection to head west toward the apartments that were located across the street from the community college.

"There's a small common area with food and vending machines." She frowned, trying to remember the last time she'd been on the small campus. It seemed like eons ago rather than a few years. "Lots of students hang out there. I think it would be a good place to start."

"Sounds good to me. I'd like to bring Rocky." At her surprised look, he quickly added, "It's not that I think he'll alert on Eli's scent, but he can be a conversation starter. You'd be surprised at how he attracts attention."

"I can imagine." She tried to smile. "I'll take anything we can get."

He nodded, then reached for her hand. They were wearing gloves, but she clung to his fingers anyway. "We're going to find Eli today. I can feel it."

She wanted to share his conviction but couldn't seem to push the heavy cloak of depression aside. "I hope so."

He squeezed her hand, then released it. They drove in silence for several minutes. Rocky shifted a bit in the back, and she imagined the dog was tired of being confined to his crate. When they reached the college, Chase headed to the farthest corner of the parking lot for a space that would accommodate the SUV and the snow machine trailer.

He released the hatch. Rocky didn't hesitate to jump down. She slid out and waited for Chase to give Rocky some water. The K9 still wore his vest, which meant Chase still had him in work mode. When they were ready, they walked across the parking lot to the building.

The common area wasn't that busy, only about six tables were occupied. Maybe it was a little too early for many students to be hanging around. A table of four girls looked at Rocky in awe.

"What kind of dog is he?" one of them asked.

Chase smiled. "This is Rocky. He's a Norwegian Elkhound. They were originally bred in Norway as hunting dogs." He glanced down at his K9 partner. "They are great trackers but can also be a bit stubborn."

"Like his master." She managed a smile as she stepped forward to join the conversation.

Chase's smile widened. "Can't deny it."

"So he tracks things? Like animals?" another girl asked.

"His ancestors did that, but Rocky tracks people now for the most part." He eyed the four girls. "Do any of you know George Twofeathers?"

"No, why? Is he missing?" The third girl's eyes widened with interest.

"Not really, we're just looking for him," she hastened to clarify. "We heard he lived around here. Maybe in the apartments across the street?"

The girls looked at each other, then shrugged. "I don't know him, sorry."

"Me either," the others chimed in.

"Thanks for your time." Chase moved on to the next table. The young couple holding hands claimed they'd never heard of George either.

By the time they'd finished in the commons, Wyn was

feeling more depressed than ever. "This was a waste of time."

"You never know." Chase shrugged as he held the door for her. "Word travels fast. Maybe someone at the apartments will have heard we're looking for George and approach us when we get there."

She sighed. "I know you're trying to be optimistic, but we could be giving George too much credit. I don't think anyone with a criminal background would be with college students. Maybe we should change our approach and head over to the Silver Spur. At least we know George likes to drink beer."

"Let's check the apartments first." Chase shrugged. "I mean, why not? We're here and you had a point about George and his mother, Regina, not being homeowners. If they live in this area, the apartments are a likely spot to find them."

"Okay." She forced a nod. "I guess I was hoping someone would have recognized his name here at the school."

He put his arm around her shoulder for a quick side hug. "I'm sure we'll find someone who knows him. There aren't that many people living in the area."

She did her best to shake off the keen sense of despair. Chase was right. They could do this. Riverton wasn't that large. Someone would know George. Or his mother, Regina.

As they headed across the street to the apartment building, her gaze narrowed on the squad parked on the street. "The tribal police are here!"

"I see that." Chase quickened his pace. "Maybe they found Regina."

She lifted her gaze to the sky in a silent prayer for the Lord to protect their son. Then she followed Chase up to the front door of the building. The door wasn't locked, so they walked right inside.

They stood for a moment listening. Then she heard the murmur of voices coming from above. "Upstairs." She turned toward the staircase.

Chase snagged her arm, holding her back. "Let me go first with Rocky."

She realized there was a slim chance Eli was upstairs. "Okay, but hurry."

"Are you ready?" Chase bent to ruffle Rocky's fur. "Search! Search for Eli!"

The dog lifted his nose and sniffed. She was a little surprised Chase took the stairs to the second floor; she knew he normally wouldn't lead Rocky in a specific direction. Then again, they were here to test Regina Twofeathers, if that's who the police were questioning.

And they must be doing just that. As they took the stairs, the voices in the hallway grew loud enough to be heard clearly.

"I haven't seen him," a woman's voice said flatly. "I kicked him out months ago."

"Are you sure about that? This is the address he gave his parole officer," one of the tribal cops said. "He's supposed to be living here with you."

"Not my fault." The woman almost sounded bored with the conversation. "He was drinking too much, so I told him to leave."

"If that's true, we can arrest him for violating the rules of his parole agreement," the cop said.

"Go ahead. I don't care."

The officers turned as Chase and Rocky approached. Rocky was still sniffing but didn't seem to have caught Eli's scent. The taller of the two cops scowled. "What are you doing here?"

"I'd like to make sure Eli isn't being held here on the premises." Chase turned toward the woman she knew must be Regina. "Ma'am, would you mind if Rocky takes a look around your apartment?"

"I have nothing to hide." Regina's broad face remained stoic. "But as I told these officers, I don't know where my son is."

"I understand." Chase gestured to his dog. "Search! Search for Eli!"

The tribal police officers watched skeptically as Rocky lowered his nose to the floor and sniffed along the hallway to the opening of Regina's apartment. The woman stepped back to give the dog room to work.

But it was soon apparent Eli had never been there. Rocky sniffed with interest, then turned and trotted back out into the hallway, moving farther down the row of apartment doors as if determined to win his game.

"Thank you for your cooperation," Chase said as he took a few steps away from the door to follow his K9. "It's helpful for us to know Eli hasn't been here."

"I told you that." Regina leveled a hard stare as she reached for the door.

"Excuse me. I'm Eli's mother." Wyn quickly stepped forward. "Do you have any idea where George might be? Who his friends are? Does he have a particular hang out?"

The shorter officer scowled. "We're asking the questions here."

She whirled to face him. "My son has been missing for eighteen hours. I'm angry and upset and willing to do whatever it takes to find him."

There was a long moment of silence before Regina

spoke. "George once came here with his friend Tyler. I don't know his last name because I didn't ask."

Chase gave her a slight nod of encouragement as he followed Rocky.

She ignored the tribal police, focusing on Regina. "Thank you. Do you know where they might be now?"

"As I said earlier, I do not." Regina began to close the door, hesitated, then said, "I hope you find your son."

"Me too." She stood for a minute staring at the closed door. Then she turned to look at the tribal police. "I apologize if I've intruded on your case."

The taller of the two shrugged. "I don't blame you for wanting to find your son. But you should leave searching for George Twofeathers to us."

Yeah, there was no way that was going to happen. But she didn't tell them that. She stepped aside to wait for Chase and Rocky. It may have been her imagination, but it seemed as if Rocky was frustrated at not finding his quarry. He stopped and sniffed at just about every door but never alerted on Eli's scent.

She knew that if Eli had been in Regina's apartment, the dog would have told them. Too bad there wasn't a way to take Rocky to every single house in the entire city to find him.

It was disheartening to know they were no closer to finding Eli than they were earlier that morning.

～

"YOU WANT something to eat or not?" Smelly Man stared at Eli in the rearview mirror, and he could almost hear his mommy telling him to use his words.

He squeezed his black stuffed horse tightly, and whispered, "Yes."

"Three breakfast sandwiches," Smelly Man said through his open window. A voice told them to drive around, so the smelly man did.

Cold air blew in through the smelly man's open window. His nose runned again, so he swiped it on his sleeve. Smelly Man scowled and tossed something into the back seat. "Use a napkin, kid."

Eli blew his nose. The napkin wasn't hard like the building block. He wanted his building block.

The woman at the window frowned at him. Had he done something wrong? He swiped at his nose again with the napkin, then held it up toward the window. The wind snatched it from his fingers, and he quickly ducked his head, hoping he wouldn't get in trouble.

As the smelly man paid for their food, he squeezed his horsey.

Soft. Soft. Soft.

"Here, take this." Smelly Man held out a sandwich. Eli took it, but it was hot to his fingers. He dropped it in his lap and put his hands on the window beside him.

Hot and cold. Hot and cold.

He stared out the window, thinking about his mommy. She hadn't found him yet, but he knew she would.

Hot and cold.

∽

"COME ON, ROCK." Chase waited for the officers to leave before leading his dog down the stairs to the main floor of the apartment building. He'd briefly considered having Rocky check the entire place, then decided that would be a fruitless endeavor. The two places Rocky had alerted on Eli's scent had been houses, not apartments.

Too many people may have noticed these guys hiding a small child here. Plus, he rather doubted George Twofeathers would have picked a place so close to his mother.

A mother who had come across as if she had washed her hands of the young man.

He couldn't imagine doing that with his own son, but he could remember the trouble he'd gotten into during his teenage years. Nothing as criminal as armed robbery, but sneaking out of the ranch to attend drinking parties and stealing some of his mom's petty cash.

Which considering how much money his parents had left behind in their trust after their deaths, he figured she'd never missed the money he'd stolen. Not that it was an excuse to do something like that.

The tribal police officers were waiting outside their squad. The taller of the two, Officer Wells, pushed away from the car to approach. "I take it your dog did not alert anywhere in the building?"

"Correct. He did not." Chase wondered if this guy had been involved six months ago after Alecia had gone missing. "Have you located Carl Longfoot yet?"

"No." Officer Wells's eyes bored into his. "I hope you don't plan to interfere with the investigation."

Chase wanted to point out that other than interviewing Regina Twofeathers, the police hadn't come up with much of anything helpful over the past eighteen hours. But he managed to keep his tone neutral. "Don't blame us for wanting to find Eli."

"You seem to be taking this case personally." The shorter

of the two cops joined them. His name tag identified him as Donner. Chase noticed the men had steered clear of Wynona after her mama bear response outside of Regina's door.

"I think everyone on this reservation should be taking this case personally." Chase scowled. "A child is missing, and we need to find him before—" He stopped, unwilling to think about his son ending up dead like Alecia.

"Ah, yes, you were here searching for Alecia." Officer Wells nodded sagely. "I remember now."

"Yes, I was." He couldn't very well deny it. "So you can understand why we are anxious to find Eli."

"Rumor has it the child is yours," Officer Donner said.

Chase tried to hide his shock. "Who told you that?"

Donner shrugged, his expression nonchalant. "Whispers across the rez, that's all."

Inwardly reeling, he turned from the officers. He'd assumed that since Wynona hadn't told him he was Eli's father, that nobody else knew the truth too.

Apparently, that was not the case.

Wynona looked impatient as she stood near the side of the road. He and Rocky crossed over to join her. She gestured toward the cops. "Let me guess, they want us to stay away?"

"Something like that." He took her arm as they walked the width of the parking lot to reach his SUV. "Who knows that I'm Eli's biological father?"

"What?" Her dark eyes widened in shock. Then she glanced over her shoulder at the cops. "I haven't told anyone about you being Eli's father. Why? What did they say?"

"There are rumors circulating through the rez that I'm Eli's father." He stopped near the back of the SUV and turned to face her. "Be honest with me for once. People are talking, and I want to know who knows about us."

Her cheeks flushed at his attack on her integrity. She set her jaw. "Obviously, my father knows, and I am sure Shana has figured it out too. But I can assure you my father wouldn't be spreading rumors about us. He was not at all happy with me when he discovered I was pregnant with your child."

The man who'd refused his request to marry Wynona. "He would if he thought it would get me in trouble."

She rolled her eyes. "That's ridiculous. Besides, I haven't even told my father Eli is missing, so why would he try to make you look bad? Can we please head over to the Silver Spur? Standing in the freezing cold and arguing over rumors won't help us find our son."

He managed a curt nod and opened the back hatch for Rocky. After making sure the dog was settled in, he stepped back and closed it again. Wyn had already climbed into the passenger seat. He paused before opening the driver's side door, wondering why the tribal officer's comment had thrown him for a loop.

Probably because it seemed as if he were the last to know. Well, except for the rest of his siblings. He slid in behind the wheel, turned the engine on, then looked at Wyn. "My family doesn't know anything about me being Eli's father."

"I understand your concern." She stared down at her hands for a moment, then met his gaze. "I don't think the rumors will extend to your ranch. And for now, I would really like to check the Silver Spur."

He fastened his seat belt and put the car into gear, doing his best to mask the flash of bitterness. "Yeah, okay." He pulled out of the parking spot and headed back toward the downtown area of the city. "But I'm going to call them soon. My family deserves to hear the truth from me, not someone who happens to be driving from the reservation up through Cody."

Wyn looked like she might argue, but then shrugged. "Whatever you think is best."

He fought back the urge to lash out at her. They wouldn't be in this predicament if she hadn't kept Eli a secret for the past four and a half years. Yet even as that thought reverberated through his mind, he knew it was useless to dwell on the past.

The trip to the Silver Spur was made in complete silence. The bar was open for business, and there were several cars in the lot despite the early hour. He had to go around the block to find a place where he could park the SUV and the trailer. There was no sign of the white truck they'd noticed late last night, and he was angry with himself for not asking the tribal police if they were still searching for it.

Not that it mattered. As far as he could tell, the tribal police were doing their best with their limited resources. He was glad the FBI was involved.

"Are you going to ask Rocky to search for Eli's scent?" Wyn asked, breaking the silence.

He shook his head. "No, but I'll bring him inside. The SUV is designed to keep him warm, but I'm hoping that when the people inside realize we're looking for a lost little boy, they'll be more apt to cooperate."

"Okay." She pushed her door open and hopped out.

Chase decided to leave Rocky's vest on. It was just another way to convince the locals to talk. He held the door open for Wynona. She entered the bar without hesitation, quickly scanning the interior.

The inside appeared to be in better shape than the worn exterior. The bar was only half full, but there were many people sitting at the various tables. The crowd was mostly Native Americans. Several of the patrons turned to look at them as they made their way across the room. Maybe it was his imagination, but Chase sensed they were more interested in him than his dog. Because he was white and didn't belong?

Wynona walked up to the group of men seated at the bar. "Excuse me, my name is Wynona Blackhorse, and I'm looking for a man by the name of George Twofeathers. Have you seen him recently?"

"George?" One of the men lifted his glass. "Here's to George." He took a long swallow of his beer.

Wyn managed to keep her smile in place. "Do you know George? Has he been in recently?"

"Nah, I haven't seen George in a few days." The more sober of the men turned to look at her. "You might want to try Albert's place."

"Albert who?" Wyn pounced on the information.

"Here's to Albert," the first man said, taking another long drink of his beer. Chase could tell Wyn was getting annoyed and stepped closer to help her out.

"Can you give us Albert's last name?" he asked. "It's really important we find George Twofeathers, so any information you can provide would be helpful."

"Pretty sure it's Son'ja, Albert Son'ja."

"Where can we find Albert?" Wyn asked. "Is he a regular? Will he be in anytime soon?"

"Here's to Albert," the first guy repeated.

The guy next to him elbowed him sharply. "Knock it off. You already did Albert."

"What's your name?" The guy still held his glass up. "I gotta drink to someone."

"Please tell me where we might find Albert Son'ja," Wyn repeated. "My son is missing, and George may know something important."

"Albert lives in a trailer on Lemon Road," the seemingly sober guy said. "It's a white trailer with black shutters."

"Thank you." Wyn looked relieved to have another lead.

Chase had noticed that the bartender had stayed far away as she'd asked her questions. Almost as if he knew George and Albert too. He nodded at the guy, then moved to an open seat at the bar.

For a long moment, the bartender pretended to be busy. Chase waited him out. Finally, the bartender looked up. "What are you drinking?"

"I'm not. I think you know that we're looking for George Twofeathers," he said. "I'd like to know why you're not willing to tell us where we can find him."

The bartender's gaze slid away. "I don't know much about George. He comes in sometimes, but that's all. I can't help you."

"Can't or won't?" Chase leaned forward. "A kid is missing, and withholding information is against the law."

The bartender shrugged. "I told you I don't know where he is."

Chase wanted to reach across the bar to grab the guy by the shirt and to shake the truth out of him. Before he could move, Wynona stepped forward.

"My father is Ogima Blackhorse. He is an important man on the tribal council. I believe he and the other tribal leaders decide which bars are approved for selling liquor."

She leaned toward the bartender as if she was about to share some secret. "I am sure you would want my father to know how helpful you've been in our search for George Twofeathers and his friend Albert."

After a long second, the bartender finally looked up. "I don't know where George is. Or Albert for that matter. But I know he was here three nights ago, bragging about how he got some special job that was going to pay him a lot of money."

"Did he say who hired him?" Chase asked. "Or anything specific about what this job entailed?"

The bartender shook his head. "Nah. But I know he must have gotten some of that cash up front because he bought a round for the bar for the first time ever."

"Do you think he's working this special job with Albert Son'ja?" Wyn asked.

"I don't know. He never mentioned a name, just that he was excited to have a decent-paying job." The bartender shrugged and looked at Wyn. "Albert wasn't here that night that he was celebrating."

"Do you remember anything else about that night?" Chase asked.

"No." The bartender looked at Wyn as if Chase wasn't worth his time. "I've told you everything I know."

"Thank you. I appreciate that. And I'll make sure my father knows too." She turned away and tipped her head toward the front door. He understood she was ready to leave.

"Thank you," Chase repeated before following her out. Rocky looked a little disappointed that he hadn't been asked to play the search game.

"Soon, buddy," Chase murmured to the dog as he

opened the hatch of the SUV for his K9 to hop in. "You're going to be back at work very soon."

"I feel like we should tell the tribal police about Albert," Wyn said as they were once again back on the road.

"We will, as soon as we verify the guy is home." A surge of adrenaline hit hard. Their search for Eli may soon be over.

11

Wynona didn't bother checking the tribal registry for Albert's name since the bartender had already provided directions to his residence. She wanted to believe they'd find Eli at Albert's home, but when Chase drove past, the place appeared deserted. Still, she clung to a thread of hope that they'd find something that would break the case wide open. There was no car in the driveway. She frowned. "I wonder if Albert drives a white pickup truck."

"Good point." Chase used the hands-free function to call Doug Bridges. When his friend answered, Chase got right to the point. "Can you ask your tech buddy to look up the DMV records for a man named Albert Son'ja? Oh, and include Regina Twofeathers as well. I need to know if either of them owns a white pickup truck."

"Sure. I'll call you back in a few," Doug agreed.

"Thanks." Chase ended the call.

"Why Regina?" she asked.

"George doesn't own a car, but his mother might. The

tribal police didn't ask her about it, and I didn't think of it until now."

"I see." She fell silent.

Chase didn't pull over near Albert's house. When she glanced at him questioningly, he shrugged. "I'm going to park a few blocks away. It's better to give Rocky a little room to pick up Eli's scent."

She understood his concern. Even if Eli wasn't being held inside the house, the little boy could have been in the driveway or on one of the side streets as they swapped cars. She silently prayed this would work. "I hope he finds something."

"Me too." Chase found a spot to pull over. He turned in his seat to face her. "Rocky and I can handle this. There's no reason for you to be out in the cold."

"I'm coming." While it was nice of him to consider her comfort, she couldn't sit there wondering if Rocky alerted on Eli's scent. "Do we wait for Doug to call back?"

"No, let's put Rocky to work." He pushed out of his driver's side door. "If I can't answer his call, he'll leave a message."

She was eager to see what Rocky might find, so she simply nodded and slid out of the car. The wind was brutal, but she ignored the icy chill. Too many hours had passed since Eli had been taken.

"Are you ready to work? Are you?" Chase went through his now familiar routine of getting Rocky revved up to search. In her opinion, the dog didn't need much encouragement, he seemed to like the game.

She stood back, watching the man she'd once loved work with his K9. The way they struggled for the upper hand was amusing. Chase offered Rocky the scent bag, but he barely sniffed it. Chase then poured some water into a collapsible bowl, and the dog turned his head away in disdain, making Chase sigh. "You're killing me, Rock. You know that, right?"

The dog wagged his high curvy tail as if in agreement.

"Okay, let's do this." Chase stepped back and threw his arm wide, his expression tense. "Search! Search for Eli!"

This was a side of Chase she'd never seen. He'd always loved being outside in nature, making his living as a hunting and fishing guide, but this was different. She liked the idea that he and his siblings offered their search and rescue services to those in need.

Like her. Shame and regret washed over her for not telling Chase about his son.

Rocky lifted his nose to the air, then set off at a trot. She and Chase quickly followed. The K9 didn't seem to have a set destination in mind, and when he headed in the opposite direction of Albert Son'ja's house, her heart sank.

Was this going to be another dead end?

Rocky moved between houses without regard for property boundaries. He eventually made his way back in the general direction of Albert's house but didn't alert.

She was about to suggest heading back to the SUV when Rocky abruptly swerved and took off in the opposite direction. Chase took off after him, and she put on a burst of speed to keep up.

Following Rocky was reminiscent of the last time the dog had found Eli's scent on the building block outside the last house. Hope bloomed in her chest as she watched Rocky moving from side to side, his nose to the ground. Every so often the dog would slow down and lift his nose to the air before continuing.

She caught up to Chase. "Do you think Rocky has found something?"

"I'm not sure." Chase's answer was noncommittal, but his expression remained tense. "We'll find out sooner or later."

Rolling her eyes, she resisted the urge to smack him. No kidding they'd find out sooner or later. She wanted to hear some sort of affirmation that Rocky had locked onto Eli's scent.

The dog turned and darted between two houses. Beyond that was a busier road. In the distance, she could see the sign for a fast-food restaurant. It made her wonder if the kidnappers were feeding Eli.

Or if Eli had even told them he was hungry.

Rocky slowed his pace, his nose working as he sniffed the air. Then he headed toward a gentle slope topped with evergreen bushes. He sniffed them for a long minute. Then he turned to look at Chase, sat, and let out a sharp bark.

His alert!

"What did you find, boy?" Chase approached the area with a slight frown furrowed in his brow. She understood his concern, as she didn't see anything at first either.

Then Chase dropped to a crouch. "Is this what you've found Rock?"

She peered over his shoulder. "What is it?"

"Looks like a crumpled napkin that's been caught in the branches."

Her heart thumped with anticipation. Now she could see it too. The white napkin was hard to see as it was snagged on the bush close to the ground covered in snow. Interesting that the napkin appeared mostly dry. Maybe because it hadn't been there for very long? Or was that more wishful thinking on her part? She kept her tone even with an effort. "Can you tell if there's some sort of logo on it? Maybe we can track down where the napkin came from."

"I can try." He disentangled it from the shrubbery. Using his gloved hands, he turned the wadded napkin over to examine it on all sides. "I don't see anything. It looks like a plain napkin that could have come from anywhere."

She frowned. It appeared rather innocuous now that she could see it more clearly, and despite her faith in Chase and Rocky, she had to ask. "Are you sure that napkin contains Eli's scent?"

Chase shrugged. "Rocky is rarely wrong." He carefully dropped the crumpled napkin into his coat pocket. "I don't have evidence bags. We should get this to Griff's team. Maybe they can run the DNA to prove it was used by Eli." He stood and grinned at his dog. "Good boy, Rock! Good boy!" He tossed the red ball high into the air. Rocky leaped up to grab it, then ran in circles with his prize.

Remembering her son's runny nose, she could easily see him using the napkin to swipe at it. But how had the napkin gotten way out here? She scanned the area again. Was Eli being held close by?

They were at least five blocks from Albert's house. "Do you think Eli was at Albert's house until he was moved down this street?" She gestured behind them. "I noticed Rocky passed it along the way. Maybe the scent of the napkin was stronger than whatever scent was left behind back there."

"Good question. We'll check the place out with Rocky to make sure he didn't miss a chance to identify the scent." Chase swept his gaze over the area. "I wonder if we should ask the various fast-food places if they've seen Eli."

She had considered that possibility too. Once again, they'd come so close to finding Eli only to come up empty-handed. She didn't want to wait for the DNA results. She was still clinging to Chase's comment about finding Eli today.

Not tomorrow, or the next. *Today.*

"I like that idea." She didn't see a downside in asking around. Other than getting the evidence to Griff, they didn't have another avenue to pursue. "After we have Rocky check Albert's house."

"Okay, let's go." He turned toward his dog. "Rocky, heel!"

The dog ignored him. Chase stood his ground, waiting, and the K9 finally trotted toward him. When Chase held out his hand for the ball, the dog dropped it on the ground six inches away.

She bit her lip as Chase sighed and bent to retrieve the ball. "That's it," he muttered. "When we're finished here, we're doing more training exercises. You hear me, Rocky? You hate training exercises."

The dog didn't seem to care, wagging his tail as they turned to retrace their steps. When they reached the street where Albert's white trailer house with the black shutters was located, Chase stopped and bent toward his dog.

"Are you ready? Are you?" Chase injected enthusiasm into his tone. "Search! Search for Eli!"

Rocky tilted his head to the side as if asking why he was playing the same game again so soon, but then he turned to lift his nose to the air. After a long second, the dog moved forward, making his usual zigzag pattern.

But when Rocky went directly past Albert's house, Wyn realized this was the end of the road. Rocky hadn't alerted, and it was clear that Eli hadn't been there.

"That's okay, Rocky. Good boy." Chase didn't offer the red ball reward. He turned. "Come, Rock."

The trip to the SUV didn't take long, but she was shivering by the time she climbed inside. Chase noticed and started the car for her using his key fob. The initial warmth from their mad dash to finding the crumpled napkin had worn off, leaving her feeling chilled to the bone.

And somewhat depressed as she'd hoped for more.

Turning in her seat, she noticed Chase was taking some extra time with Rocky, examining his paws before stepping back to close the hatch.

"Is he okay?" She glanced back at Rocky as he slid in behind the wheel.

"Yeah, just checking. We were gone longer than I anticipated, and I wanted to be sure there weren't bits of ice or salt between his pads." Chase offered a wry grin. "Maya's K9, Zion, uses booties without complaint, but no surprise, Rocky hates them." He held his hands toward the heating vents, and it made her feel better to know he was feeling the cold too. "I try to avoid using them if possible."

"I thought K9s were supposed to be well trained." She arched a brow. "Seems like Rocky doesn't listen as well as he should."

"Tell me about it." Chase shook his head. "When I adopted Rocky, I didn't realize Elkhounds were known to be stubborn and independent. Yet he's an amazing tracker. I'm encouraged by the way he alerted so often on Eli's scent."

"Yes, me too." She did her best to shake off the cloak of despair. Before she could say anything, Chase's phone rang. The name on his dashboard computer screen identified the caller as Doug.

"Hey, Doug," Chase answered. "What did Ian find?"

"No white truck for either of those names," Doug said. "Do you have any other known associates?"

"Unfortunately, we don't." Chase looked dejected at the news. "Thanks anyway."

"You know, Ian is still working the ancestry angle," Doug

said. "I don't think he's found anything related to that first name you gave me, Julia Stone. I've asked him to add Regina Twofeathers to the mix."

"Have him include a George Twofeathers too," Chase said.

"And Carl Longfoot," she chimed in. "Regina, Carl, and George are the names of people we know for sure are connected in some way to Eli's disappearance. Either as a willing participant or guilt by association."

"Will do," Doug agreed. "If you need anything else, let me know."

"Thanks." Chase ended the call. "Should we contact Griff about the napkin? Or head over to the fast-food restaurants to ask around about Eli ourselves?"

"Fast-food restaurants." She gestured toward the sign that was barely visible in the distance. "Maybe it's wishful thinking on my part, but I'm hoping these guys care enough about Eli to feed him. And if they used a drive-through, maybe someone will remember seeing him. I still believe that people here on the rez will be more likely to talk to me as Eli's mother than to the FBI."

"Sounds like a plan." Chase put the vehicle into gear and circled the block so that they were headed in the correct direction.

As they grew closer to the main street winding through town, she noticed there were two restaurants within a half mile. One was by far the more popular, and she wondered if the kidnappers might have avoided that one on purpose.

Then again, she wasn't sure what these kidnappers were thinking. There still wasn't a ransom demand, and she couldn't understand what they were waiting for.

Chase pulled into the small parking lot of the closest one, finding a long empty space to park the SUV and the trailer. As Wyn opened her door, she glanced up at the sunny sky and silently prayed.

Please, Lord, guide us to Eli! Please? We need to find him before it's too late.

AFTER PARKING the car and trailer, Chase decided to leave Rocky in the SUV. The dog had done a great job that morning and was currently stretched out on his side, asleep. There was no reason to take him inside. He left the SUV engine running, hoping they wouldn't be too long.

He'd have to stop for gas again very soon. Hauling the trailer was wreaking havoc with his mileage. He could pretty much watch the needle of the gas gauge tick down toward empty with every mile.

He opened the door for Wyn, then hung back as she took the lead.

There was no doubt Griff wouldn't be happy to learn they'd questioned the local fast-food restaurants, but he sensed Wynona was right about her ability to convince her fellow Native Americans to cooperate with finding their son. As far as Chase was concerned, this was a circumstance in which it was better to apologize afterward than to request permission.

"Excuse me," Wynona said. "I'm looking for my little boy, Eli. He was taken last night without my consent." Her carefully worded statement alluded to the fact that the child's father may have been the one to take him. "I'm wondering if anyone has seen a man traveling with a small boy? Eli is four and a half but tall for his age."

"I have not," the young man behind the counter said.

Then he turned, and asked, "Has anyone seen a man with a kid?"

A chorus of negative responses came from the others. Wyn's smile faltered, but she nodded. "Thank you very much. If you do see a man with a little boy who doesn't seem to belong to him, will you please call the tribal police?"

This request was met with silence. Finally, one woman said, "Yes, if we see anything suspicious, we will call the police."

"Thank you." Wyn turned and grimaced as she joined him near the door. "I don't think they're lying to me, but did you notice how they froze when I mentioned calling the tribal police?"

"Oh yeah, they didn't like that." He held the door for her. "Maybe we'll have better luck at the next place."

"Maybe." She didn't look convinced. It was clear the lackluster response to her request to notify the tribal police bothered her.

He drove the short distance to the next chain restaurant. This one had more cars in the parking lot, forcing him to find someplace to park out on the street. For the millionth time, he wondered if he'd been foolish to drag the trailer around the city. So far, the areas where Rocky alerted to Eli's scent had all been near streets. Not out in the wilderness.

Better to be overprepared than not, he thought with a sigh.

Again, he left the motor running and Rocky in the back. The dog seemed content now that he'd won the search game. At least for now.

He and Wyn went inside and had to wait in line to speak to anyone. The young woman at the register looked harried. "What do you want?"

"Have you noticed a man with a little boy buying food

this morning?" When the woman stared at her blankly, Wyn added, "Like maybe the little boy didn't look happy to be there?"

The woman gave her an exasperated look. "I've been here since six in the morning. I have no idea how many customers I've served."

"Could we speak to a manager?" Chase asked. "This is really important. We're searching for a missing child."

"Just a minute." The girl turned to scan the workers. "Rose? These people want to speak to a manager."

"I'll be there soon," a voice replied. From where Chase stood, he couldn't see the woman. She appeared to be making burgers.

He tugged Wyn aside so the next person in line could place their order. As busy as this place was, he doubted anyone would have noticed a man with an unusually quiet young boy buying food.

Wyn gnawed on her lower lip. "I wonder if we should ask the drive-through clerk? If the restaurant was crowded, he may not have brought Eli inside."

He wasn't sure how to respond. The minutes ticked by slowly until a round woman with her dark hair pulled into a tight bun came toward them. "I'm the manager," she said. "What's wrong with your food?"

"Oh, nothing. Sorry about that." Wyn managed a smile. "My name is Wynona, and my four-and-a-half-year-old son was taken last night without my permission. The man who has him may have come by to buy food for him earlier today."

Rose frowned. "As you can see, we're pretty busy." She gestured toward the hustle and bustle of the restaurant workers. "I've been here since we opened this morning. I can't say that anything unusual about our customers comes to mind."

"I understand and appreciate that. Would you be so kind as to ask your other employees if they noticed anything unusual?" Wyn asked. "I know I'm asking a lot, but I'm running out of options."

Rose stared at Wynona for a long minute. "I don't think that will help. Unless the child was screaming in terror, I doubt anyone would notice."

Wyn's shoulders slumped. Chase gestured to the drive-through window. "Maybe just check with the drive-through staff? We don't know that he actually came inside, but maybe one of them noticed something?"

"Please," Wyn added. "I haven't seen my son in eighteen hours, and I'm terrified something bad has happened to him."

Rose sighed heavily. "I am a mother too. For you, I'll ask. Wait here." She turned and made her way back through the kitchen area.

Chase put his arm around Wyn's waist. "If this doesn't work, we can try other restaurants in the area. Maybe that napkin traveled farther than we realize."

She leaned against him for a moment. "I know. But we may be on the wrong track. The napkin could have been stuck on that bush since last night. Or maybe the napkin was in the car for a while. It could be they haven't stopped recently for a meal at all."

He hated to admit she was right. Then he noticed the manager, Rose, was hovering near the woman working the drive-through window. After a few minutes, the two women spoke briefly. Then the manager turned to look at them.

Another few minutes passed, then the manager took the headset from the drive-through worker's hands and put it in place. Rose began to take orders as the other worker snaked her way through the restaurant to meet with them.

"My name is Mary. I understand you're looking for a man with a little boy who might not be his own?" she asked warily.

"Yes, my son is about four and a half. Did you see something unusual?" Wyn asked.

"Maybe." The worker hesitated. "A man came through about an hour and a half ago; he had a little boy in the back seat. I noticed because the child wasn't in a booster seat as he should have been at that age."

Chase's pulse kicked into high gear. He glanced at Wynona who had removed her gloves and was swiping at her phone.

"Did the little boy look like this?" Wynona turned the screen toward her. "He would have been wearing a dark-blue coat?"

Mary nodded slowly. "Yes, actually, that does look like him." She frowned. "I must say the boy didn't look scared or upset. If not for the fact that he wasn't in a booster seat, I wouldn't have noticed anything amiss. He didn't say a word the whole time."

The first sighting of Eli and his kidnapper! Chase couldn't believe their hunch had paid off. He reached for his phone. It was time to call Griff and get the FBI here right away.

Eli's kidnapper had been there less than thirty minutes ago. They couldn't have gone far. And maybe, just maybe Mary could help them find him.

12

Eli was alive and relatively unharmed! When Wyn's knees threatened to buckle, she kept herself upright with an effort. This wasn't the time to fall apart. They hadn't found him yet, but the relief at knowing Eli was recently identified in the back seat of a truck and had been provided something to eat kept a large chunk of her panic at bay.

"He wasn't crying? Or looked hurt?" she asked.

"Not at all," Mary assured her. "Like I said, I might not have noticed if not for the fact that he wasn't in a booster seat. I remember thinking the boy's father should know better."

"He's not Eli's father." Wyn lightly grasped Mary's arm. "Can you describe the man? And his vehicle?"

Mary scrunched up her forehead. "I don't remember the truck, other than to notice it was a pickup truck with one of those narrow back seats." At her frown, Mary added, "You know, not a full cab but a half of one."

"What color was the truck?" Wyn was desperate for

more. "Did you notice anything else inside? Or outside? Stickers?"

"I think the truck was white," Mary said. "Maybe silver? Light for sure, not dark. And I'm sorry, I don't remember anything else about it. Or the guy driving. He looked average as far as his weight. His age?" She looked thoughtful. "I'd guess his mid-twenties."

George Twofeathers. She turned toward Chase who was texting on his phone. "We need a picture to show her."

"Working on that," he said. "Griff is on his way." He lifted his head to smile at Mary. "We really appreciate your help on this."

"Of course." Mary looked concerned. "If I had known the child was in danger, I'd have done more."

"You couldn't have known." Wyn tried to come up with more questions. "Did you happen to notice what the driver wore? The color of his coat?"

"Dark, maybe black or blue." Mary lifted her hands, palms upward. "I only took his money and handed him his food. The entire interaction didn't take long."

"I know, and I'm sorry to keep pestering you." Wyn tried to smile. "It's just that you're the only person who has seen my son since he was taken." Tears pricked her eyes. "I'm so relieved he's doing okay."

"I can't imagine what you're going through." Mary's tone was sympathetic.

"Does this restaurant have any security cameras?" Chase asked.

"I don't think so." Mary looked around as if the thought of cameras had never occurred to her.

"It's okay, I just thought I'd ask." Chase glanced at her. "I'm heading outside to get Rocky. Looks like we may be here a while."

"Okay." She knew they'd have to wait for the FBI agent to get there and maybe answer a few more questions, but she didn't want to stick around for long. She wanted to head out on another lead to find Eli.

"I really need to get back to work," Mary said as Chase left.

"Okay, but we'll need you to speak with the authorities once they get here." She was careful not to mention the FBI. Not that she thought Mary would refuse to cooperate, but in general, her people didn't trust the federal government. And with good reason.

"Sure." Mary hustled off, leaving Wyn standing there alone. She gazed at the drive-through window, trying to imagine how Mary had noticed Eli in the back seat of the pickup truck.

Alive and unhurt. At least physically. Inwardly? She had no idea.

Eli didn't interact with people the same way other kids did. Half of the time, Wyn didn't know what went through Eli's mind. Even when she constantly reminded him to use his words, he didn't often go into detail about his thoughts or feelings.

Maybe because he was only four and a half, but she wasn't sure he'd ever have full conversations the way she secretly hoped.

None of that mattered now. She needed her son home safe. His absence left a gaping hole in her heart that would never be filled if they didn't find him.

"Where's Mary?" Chase crossed over to join her with Rocky at his side. The dog sniffed the air with interest, and she imagined Rocky would love nothing more than a burger with the works.

"Back at the drive-through." She sighed. "How long until Griff gets here?"

"Five minutes or less." Chase glanced around the restaurant. "I took a walk outside but didn't see any cameras. That's rather unusual. Most places have them, especially near the drive-through window."

"I'm not surprised." She shrugged. "Things on the rez are different. Nobody likes the idea that big brother might be watching."

"I guess so. I did see a gas station a block or two down the road. I am sure they have cameras. I'm hoping Griff can get the owner to turn the video over. They may have gotten a glimpse of the white truck driving by."

That possibility cheered her up. "Really? It would be great if there were cameras that captured the truck. We really need a license plate."

"Yeah, that would help." He put his arm around her shoulders. "We're getting close, Wyn. I can feel it."

She desperately wanted to believe him.

When Griff arrived, he looked annoyed. "You should have called the minute Rocky alerted on the napkin."

"Here, you can take it as evidence." Chase pulled it from his pocket.

"You don't get it," Griff said irritably. "The evidence has been moved, which makes it unusable in court. I can run the DNA, but I'm not sure those results will us do any good in the long run if we can't use it."

"I don't care about the trial. Right now, I'm more concerned with finding my son." She glared at Griff. "Once we have Eli safe, then we can worry about building your case."

The agent sighed. "I understand, I do. But we need to

preserve the evidence as we go. If something happens, and Eli isn't able to testify . . ."

She blanched, realizing what he meant. If Eli was killed and they needed to press charges against these guys for kidnapping and murder.

Murder!

No, she couldn't bear to think about that. She shook her head and strove to keep her voice calm. "Mary saw Eli alive and well a half hour ago. The kidnapper bought him a breakfast sandwich. I don't know why they took him, but we're going to find him."

"Yes, we will," Griff quickly agreed. He averted his gaze, scanning the restaurant. "Okay, which of these is our witness, Mary? I have a six-pack of photos for her to look at to see if she can identify our suspect."

"Back at work." Wyn gestured to the window. "I'll ask Rose the manager to cover for her again."

Thankfully, Rose didn't balk at freeing Mary up for the second time in a few minutes. She led Mary back to the empty table Griff and Chase had found. Mary eyed Rocky warily as she approached.

"Don't worry, he's harmless." Chase smiled. "He's a search and rescue dog."

"Really?" Mary's eyes widened with interest. "That's amazing."

"I'm Special Agent Griffin Flannery." Griff rose as he introduced himself. "Thank you for agreeing to meet with me. As you know, we have a missing child, and time is of the essence. I understand you noticed Eli Blackhorse in the back of a white pickup truck?"

"Yes." If Mary was reluctant to talk to the FBI, she didn't show it. "And I only noticed because he wasn't in a booster seat."

"I understand, please sit down." When Mary glanced back at the busy restaurant, Griff added, "This won't take long."

"Okay." Mary sat next to Griff and gestured to her and Chase. "But I've told them everything I know."

Griff looked slightly frustrated, but simply nodded. "I understand, and we are grateful for your cooperation. If you could please tell your story again for my sake, I would appreciate it."

Mary complied. As she spoke, Wyn didn't notice any discrepancy in her story, which was a good sign. Griff asked questions similar to what she had.

"I just didn't pay that much attention." Mary's tone was apologetic. "As I said earlier, if I had known there was a missing child, I would have done more."

"I issued an Amber Alert." Griff grimaced. "I know that doesn't necessarily mean the tribe has been notified."

Wyn knew that several national emergency systems like the Amber Alert had not been fully expanded throughout the Native American reservations. Now, she silently vowed that once they had Eli back safe, she would personally make sure her father championed that change here within the Wind River rez.

"I have a group of photographs to show you," Griff said, breaking the silence. "I'd like you to tell me if any of these men look familiar."

He spread the photo array out on the table. Mary leaned forward to examine them. The six pictures were lined up three per line. Wyn noticed they were all Native American men who were thin and in their mid-twenties.

Mary took so long to say anything Wyn wondered if George Twofeathers wasn't the man who had Eli. That maybe his accomplice had taken over.

"Yes, this man." Mary tapped the last photo on the upper line. "This man was driving the truck with the little boy in the back seat."

"Thank you." Griff's eyes gleamed with satisfaction, and Wyn knew Mary had nailed the ID. "His name is George Twofeathers. Does that ring a bell? Do you know him? Or his mother, Regina?"

"No, I've never heard of him or his mother." Mary shot another guilty glance over her shoulder. "If that's all, I really need to get back to work."

"Yes, that's fine. You've been very helpful." Griff rose and offered his hand. After a moment, Mary took it. "Here is my card. If you see this man again, or think of anything else, please call."

"Sure." Mary tucked the card into her uniform pocket. "I hope you find him."

"We will," Griff spoke with confidence, sounding much like Chase. And while she was glad to know that George Twofeathers was the man who had Eli, the sad truth was they were still no closer to finding their son.

"YOU NEED to ask the gas station for their security video to see if you can pick out the white truck," Chase said to Griff after Mary returned to work. "Other local cameras may have video of the truck too."

"Yeah, I'm aware of how to run an investigation." Griff's tone was testy. "It would be easier if the rez would operate like the rest of the world."

"I received the Amber Alert," Chase frowned. "I didn't realize the notice wouldn't go out to everyone on the rez."

"I should have mentioned it." Wyn sighed. "To be

honest, it didn't occur to me either. Things here are still a bit medieval when it comes to technology."

Medieval was putting it mildly, but he let it go. "What else can we do?"

"Nothing." Griff stood. "I'll see what we can find on the truck. The tribal police have already put out a BOLO on George Twofeathers."

Chase stood too. His abrupt movement startled Rocky who scrambled to his feet. "There must be something we can do to help."

"I should come with you to ask for the camera video," Wyn said. "I believe the locals will cooperate with me more so than you."

Griff looked frustrated. "I can handle it. We have a missing kid, it's all hands on deck. I've asked the tribal police to assist me in getting the videos. Until we have a line on the white truck, there's nothing more you can do."

Wyn looked as if she wanted to argue, so he put a hand on her arm. "It's okay. We can drive around looking for the truck."

Griff didn't look happy to hear his plan, but didn't protest. "All I ask is that you call me if you find a lead before you go gallivanting around the rez."

Chase had no intention of making any rash promises. If they found Eli, he wouldn't sit back and wait for the feds to show up. Or the tribal police for that matter. He was still upset to have learned the Amber Alert hadn't gone out to everyone as he'd anticipated. "I called you about this lead, didn't I?"

Griff scowled. "Only after you'd done the investigation for yourself and ruined the evidence collection. Don't push me, Sullivan. Stay in touch."

"Of course." He waited for Griff to leave, then gestured to

the front counter of the restaurant. "Don't judge me, but I'm hungry. Let's grab something for the road."

Wyn hesitated only for a moment. "As odd as it sounds, I'd like that. Seems fitting to have a meal from the same place Eli did."

He walked over to stand in line. In his stubborn way, Rocky eventually followed. Chase paid for their food, then gladly took the sandwiches.

Outside, he discovered the sun was beginning to warm the air to a tolerable level. Not that it still wasn't below freezing, but something about bright sunshine gave the illusion of warmth.

Rocky was too well trained to beg for table food, but the K9 did nose the bag as they covered the distance to the street where he'd parked his SUV and trailer. Seeing the gouge along the upper edge of the trailer cover, it occurred to him that the kidnappers hadn't tried to shoot at them again.

Hopefully because they were too busy moving from one location to the next. In his opinion, it was important to keep these guys off balance.

Maybe having the Sullivan K9 logo on the car was helping rather than hindering the investigation.

After putting Rocky in the back, he slid into the driver's seat and handed Wyn the food. "Let's eat while we drive. I need to fill up the gas tank, though, before we head out of town. I'm hoping George may not have taken Eli very far."

"I like that idea." She rummaged in the bag and pulled out their meals. He'd noticed she'd gone with a breakfast sandwich, but Chase had gotten a large double cheeseburger.

He reached for her hand. "Let's take a moment to say grace. Lord Jesus, we thank You for this food and for letting us know our son, Eli, has not been physically harmed. We humbly ask that You continue to guide us so that we may bring him home. Amen."

"Amen," Wyn whispered.

The home he was referring to was the Sullivan ranch, but he kept that thought to himself. One step at a time. First, they had to find Eli.

Then the little boy would need to get to know him. How long that would take with his autism diagnosis, Chase had no clue.

But he wasn't going anywhere. If he had to temporarily move in with Wynona, he would.

He ate as they cruised the streets around the fast-food restaurant. He noticed a tribal squad parked outside at the gas station and wished he could be there to see the video footage for himself. He pulled in to fill his gas tank.

Then he had an idea.

"I have a pair of two-way radios in the snowmobile trailer." He jumped out to get the gas pump started, then reached up to open the trailer covering the snowmobiles. He kicked himself for not thinking about that sooner. He really should have asked Doug and Maya to join him. They had both been cops and probably would have thought of this right away. He hopped up onto the trailer and rummaged in the closest bag. Moving the helmet and extra warm weather gear aside, he found them.

The radios were nothing fancy, they used them to communicate while riding the sleds. Talking over the engine noise was nearly impossible. They often had to relay pertinent information regarding a search, especially if they were covering a wide area.

After leaping down from the trailer, he closed and secured the cover. Then he opened the passenger side door to hand her the radios. "We can use these to hear what the cops are saying."

"We can?" Wyn looked surprised. "Are you sure?"

He wasn't sure of anything, but it was worth a try.

He finished pumping gas, then returned to the front seat. With deft movements, he connected the cable to the adapter he used for his phone and turned on the radio. He searched the radio waves for the channel law enforcement might be using.

After long minutes of hearing nothing but static, he'd wondered if this wouldn't work after all. Then he heard voices. Not as clear as he'd have hoped, but voices.

"Looks—head—west." The statement was broken up by static.

"Did they say the truck was heading west?" Wyn asked.

"I think so." He tried to tune the radio in, but he wasn't successful. More static filled the air, then another comment.

"We'll—the BOLO," a voice said.

Wyn's hand shot out to grab his arm. "Update the BOLO? Is that what he said? Do you think they got a license plate?"

"Maybe." He considered calling Griff to find out but doubted the fed would tell him anything. He pulled back out into traffic. He couldn't fiddle with the radio while driving, so he gave it to Wyn. "I'm going to head west. See if you can get this to work better."

As she fiddled with the controls, he tried to think like George. He doubted the guy would stay on the main roads, so he brought up the map app on his phone so it would display on his dashboard computer screen. He noticed there was a side road that meandered northwest and turned to take it.

"This is the best I can do." Wyn sighed. "It's more static than not."

"Okay." The comments between the tribal police officers were few and far between, which didn't help. Within ten minutes, they had driven all the way through town and were heading deeper into the reservation. Well outside the city limits.

He began to second-guess his decision. Until now, the locations where the kidnappers had kept Eli had been in town, not outside. But maybe that had changed.

He decided they should keep going for a while. There was no sign of a white truck, which was disappointing.

If they had something belonging to George, he could ask Rocky to track him. He'd given the crumpled napkin to Griff and wished now that he hadn't.

The napkin had been in his pocket, but he wasn't sure there would be enough of a scent to use for tracking. Especially since Rocky had already alerted on the napkin while searching for Eli. There wasn't an easy way to explain to Rocky that he wanted him to follow the other scent on the napkin. Not Eli's scent.

The last thing he wanted to do was confuse his dog. Not when he'd done such a great job in searching for his son.

When they reached a fork in the road, he slowed and glanced questioningly at Wyn. "Which way?"

"I say go right. That way is still slightly northwest." She frowned. "Although I don't see much by the way of housing in either direction."

He didn't either. Fighting doubt, he turned to head northwest. There were more hills in this direction. Every so often, gusts of wind blew snow across the open areas between them. In the distance, the Tetons spiked the blue sky.

"I don't think we're going to find them way out here," Wyn said, after they'd gone several miles. "You should probably turn around."

"Okay." He had noticed the roads had gotten narrower, especially as they were well off the main highway. They'd passed the small Central Wyoming airport several miles back, and he'd wondered if it was possible the kidnappers had planned to take Eli away via a charter plane. But he hadn't wanted to worry Wyn by saying anything. "I'll have to wait for the next intersection. I need plenty of room to make the turn with the trailer."

She nodded and stared down at the radio. "If they really do have his license plate, I hope they find him soon."

Looking at the wide-open spaces around them, he wasn't sure that having a plate number would help. He hated to admit his plan to search for the white truck had been a stupid idea. George could have taken Eli anywhere in the time they'd been seen at the drive-through.

All the way to the casino or even farther.

Consulting the map, he made a note of the next intersection. "Two miles ahead, there's another fork in the road. I'll turn around there."

There were still no houses of any sort. Maybe they were wrong about George keeping off the main highway. From what he could tell via the map, some of these small roads just dead-ended in the middle of nowhere.

He slowed his speed and turned to the left at the intersection. Then he had to back up with the trailer so he could head back toward Riverton.

"Wait a minute, is there something out there?" Wyn was peering out her passenger side window.

He leaned forward to see better. At first, he didn't understand, then he realized the light from the sun was reflecting off something. "I can't tell what it is."

"Let's take a look." Wyn gestured. "We've come this far. Maybe it's a car."

"Okay." He backed up the trailer again so he could turn around. As they headed north, it soon became clear the object in the distance was a car.

A white truck.

He hit the brake. "Stay here. I'll check it out with Rocky."

"I'm coming too!" Wyn pushed on her door.

"I'm armed; you're not." He sighed, knowing he was wasting his breath. "Fine, but you stay behind me, understand? This guy could have a gun."

"I know that. I was there when they fired at us." Her expression was a mixture of hope and dread. "I can't help but think they dumped the truck to throw us off track."

He released the back hatch. Rocky eagerly jumped down. The dog had been cooped up for a while now and appeared anxious to go.

"Are you ready?" He injected excitement in his tone and decided against offering water since the dog didn't drink most of the time. Rocky still wore his vest, and his tail wagged back and forth, his dark-brown eyes on his. He offered the scent bag with Eli's clothes. "Are you ready to search? Search for Eli."

Rocky whirled and began to take in the scents. While there were no people in the area, the wildlife provided plenty of distractions. Rocky began to trot across the field in the general direction of the truck.

Chase removed the glove from his right hand and reached for his weapon. Then he quickened his pace to follow Rocky. Thankfully, Wyn stayed behind him as promised.

Rocky didn't take a straight path to the truck; he followed the scents wafting on the breeze. Chase approached cautiously, eyeing the vehicle, trying to determine whether it was empty.

When it was clear Rocky was about to alert near the truck, he called the dog back. "Rocky, heel."

Rocky stared at him. The dog wasn't used to being stopped in the middle of a search.

Chase rushed forward, holding his weapon up with two hands. "Get out of the car with your hands up!"

No answer.

He stepped closer, peering inside. He didn't see anyone in the front seat. Frowning, he moved up to the window to see into the back.

And found him. George Twofeathers's body had been shoved down on the floor between the seats.

A bullet hole marred the center of his forehead.

13

S melly Man was gone.

Eli rocked back and forth as the scary man drove the car. After he and Smelly Man had eaten their food, Scary Man had come to meet with them. Scary Man had picked Eli up and carried him to the back seat of the other car.

The car was black, like his stuffed horsey. Even though he was inside, he heard the two men shouting at each other outside. Scary Man did most of the yelling. Something about almost getting caught by the police.

Then he'd heard a loud *bang!*

Eli hadn't heard that sound before, and he didn't like it. He rocked faster, wishing for his building block. After a while, Scary Man had come back to the car and stared at him. "Behave or you're next."

Eli didn't say anything. He had been behaving. He hadn't caused any trouble. He squeezed his stuffy tight. Then he noticed there was a small metal thing next to him in the back seat. It wasn't square like his building block. It was short and narrow with a blunt tip on the end. Best of all, it was hard. The opposite of soft.

He picked it up with his free hand and immediately felt better. Hard. He liked having two things to hold in his hands.

Hard and soft. As the man drove on a bumpy road, he slowed his rocking and squeezed his hands.

Hard and soft. He still wasn't sure what was taking his mommy so long to get there. His eyes felt heavy, and he yawned. Then he stretched out on the back seat.

He was so tired.

Hard. Soft . . .

"CHASE? WHAT'S WRONG?" Wyn had promised to stay back, but the horrified expression on Chase's face filled her with dread. Was this it? Had he found Eli inside?

Was their son dead?

She rushed forward, but Chase quickly held up a hand. "It's not Eli," he said, keying into the source of her fear. "George Twofeathers is dead."

What? Wyn stopped abruptly, staring in shock. "Are you sure?"

"Oh yeah." He came toward her. "There's no mistake." When she started to move around him, he reached out a hand to stop her. "Don't, Wyn. There's no reason for you to look at him. Trust me, you don't want that image in your head."

"But why?" She grappled with knowing George had been murdered. "I don't understand. And where is Eli?"

"I wish I knew the answer to both of those questions."

Chase's expression was somber as he cupped her shoulders with his hands. "I assume George had been killed because he was viewed as a loose end. Or maybe whoever is ultimately in charge of this thing has decided his usefulness is over." He hesitated, then added, "I have to wonder if the news about Mary identifying him via the drive-through restaurant has made its way through the town rumor mill. And that's the reason George was killed."

"We just found out ourselves. How could the kidnappers have known about Mary seeing Eli?" As soon as she said the words, she thought about the bits of conversation between the tribal police that they'd overheard by using the radio. "You think the kidnapper has a two-way radio?" Another thought hit. "Or do they have an insider working for the tribal police?"

"I don't know about having an inside track with the police," Chase hastened to assure her. "I was thinking more along the lines of the radio or just rumors spreading throughout town."

She swallowed hard. "Okay, so maybe they had heard the news, but to go as far as killing someone?" The violent act made her sick to her stomach. And brought the panic back to the forefront of her mind. "I was starting to believe this is about the audit I'm doing for the tribal council. That maybe one of the members wanted to hide something illegal. But this?" She waved a hand at the white truck. "Cold-blooded murder?"

"I know." Chase drew her into his arms. She rested her forehead against his chest, trying to stay strong. Yet she couldn't shake the fear that the same person who'd brutally murdered George Twofeathers had their son.

Chase pressed a kiss to her temple. "Let's try not think the worst. We know God is watching over Eli."

She nodded, even though it was getting harder to believe that. Every time they got close to finding Eli, it turned out that he was even farther away than they'd thought.

And with George Twofeathers dead and the white truck abandoned, they had literally nothing to go on.

Nothing!

Panic clawed up her throat, threatening to choke her. She struggled to breathe.

"Let's pray." Chase bowed his head. "Dear Lord Jesus, we beg You to keep Elijah safe in Your care! Give us the strength, courage, and knowledge to find our son. Amen."

The tightness in her throat eased, just enough for her to echo, "Amen."

Rocky nudged them, as if wondering what was going on. Chase stared down at her for a long moment, then brushed a light kiss over her mouth. Then he pulled away and turned toward his dog. He threw out his arm wide. "Search! Search for Eli!"

Rocky whirled and went back to work. She frowned. "Why are asking him to do that? We already know Eli was in the white truck."

"I want to be able to reward him." Chase shrugged. "He likes to win the search game, and I want him to stay interested in finding Eli."

She nodded in understanding and watched as Rocky picked up the scent trail. He sniffed all around the truck, and she wondered if George's dead body was throwing the K9 off his game. But just a minute later, Rocky sat near the driver's side door of the truck and let out a sharp bark.

"Good boy, Rocky!" Chase praised the dog and threw the red ball for him. Rocky wagged his curly tail, then leaped up to catch the ball.

"I need to call Griff." Chase sighed heavily as watched

Rocky celebrate his win. "He and his crime scene techs need to get out here ASAP."

She nodded.

Chase pulled out his phone. Rocky still ran around for a bit, then stopped and lifted his nose into the air while still carrying the red ball in his mouth. Her heart thumped wildly in her chest at the possibility he'd alerted on Eli's scent again, but then the dog turned and trotted back to Chase.

As usual, the K9 dropped the ball several feet from Chase rather than placing it in his handler's outstretched hand.

"Griff? I'm calling with bad news. We found George Twofeathers dead from a gunshot wound to the head in the back of the white pickup truck." Chase scanned the area. "I'm not sure exactly where we are, roughly six miles past the airport. More north than west by my estimation."

She could easily imagine Griff's response. Chase's expression didn't change, though, as he continued to provide directions.

"We stayed off the main highway," he explained. "And yeah, it's not good. I wish we would have gotten here earlier." He listened some more. "Okay, we'll stick around until you get here. But you'll want your crime scene techs too." He bent his head and seemed to take note of the footprints in the snow. Something she hadn't paid attention to until now. "I think George was killed nearby or while he was inside his truck."

A wave of nausea hit hard. Had Eli witnessed the murder? She shivered.

She didn't want to stay close to the dead body. Yet this was the last place they knew for certain Eli had been.

Oh, Eli, she thought on a wave of desperation. *Where are you?*

If there was an answer, it was lost in the wind.

CHASE DIDN'T SEE any blood stains in the snow, but there were plenty of footprints that told the story of what had gone down out here in the middle of nowhere.

The only good thing was that there weren't any footprints small enough to be made by a child. He hated thinking that Eli had been in the truck during the murder, but somehow, he didn't think that was the case.

It would have been too difficult to get Eli out of the back seat after shoving George's body in there.

He felt antsy staying near the scene of George's murder. The more he thought about it, the more he realized the shooting must have happened recently. Like maybe even within the past thirty to forty minutes. They didn't know who had Eli or what kind of vehicle they were driving, but he had the sudden urge to hit the road.

"Let's go." He took a step forward to retrieve Rocky's ball. He didn't have time to assert his alpha status now.

"I thought we were waiting for Griff?"

"I changed my mind." He could not ignore the sense of urgency. "We didn't pass any vehicles on the way here, so that leads me to believe that whoever has Eli is still heading north on this road."

Wyn's eyes widened as that idea sank deep. "You think so?"

"Yeah, I do." He turned and strode toward the SUV with Wyn hurrying to follow. He used his key fob to open the rear hatch for Rocky. "Get up!"

For once, Rocky obeyed his command. He closed the hatch, then quickly went up to slide in behind the wheel.

Seconds later, they were back out on the road. Again, he wrestled with the possibility of leaving the trailer behind. But what if they needed it? Judging by the lack of homes out here, he figured they may need to go cross-country sooner or later.

And he'd rather be prepared for the inevitable. Even though pulling the trailer meant going slower. Not to mention sucking all his gas. Thankfully, he'd filled up back in Riverton. At least they could go for a while before he'd have to worry about getting more.

"Where do you think they're headed?" Wyn asked, reading his mind.

"I was hoping you'd have an idea about that." He waved his hand toward the open landscape. "Where does this road go?"

"I don't know." She sounded exasperated. "It's not as if I drive out this way on a routine basis."

"Check your map app on your phone." He tried not to sound accusatory, but this was her home, not his. And this area outside the casino had not been the focus of his search for Alecia six months ago. "If you wanted to hide a kid, where would you take him?"

She frowned and pulled off her gloves so she could work the phone. "If we turn left at the next intersection, there's a road that will take us to the casino."

He frowned, not sure the kidnapper's intent was to take that route. Wouldn't there be more people in the city housing the casino? "What if we turn right instead?"

"That takes us toward the small town of Pavillion." She nodded slowly. "Yes, I think they'd go that way rather than toward the casino."

"Okay. Then we'll head there." There was a fifty-fifty chance of guessing wrong, but he tried not to think about that. "Stay alert for vehicles. Maybe we'll catch up to them."

She set her phone in her lap and stared out her passenger window. "I wish I understood what they want with Eli. Why hasn't anyone called me to make a ransom demand? What's the point if this isn't about money?"

"I wish I knew the reasons behind this too." Chase was plagued by those thoughts as well. More so now that George Twofeathers had been callously murdered and stuffed in the back of his truck. Whoever had arranged this kidnapping was not joking around. "When did you plan to finish your audit?"

"I told the tribal council the audit would take three weeks to complete, and I only started two days ago." The color leeched from her cheeks. "You don't think they plan to keep Eli for three weeks?"

"I don't know what to think." He had no idea what the driving force was behind the kidnapping. "The audit is the only thing that makes sense. Nothing else has changed, right?" He glanced at her. "I can't imagine you've done something else that might cause someone to take such a drastic action."

"No. Just the audit. I'll call my father now and resign my position." Her face turned stoic. "They can find someone else to do the audit."

He wasn't sure what to say about that. Normally, he wouldn't recommend making snap decisions during a time of crisis, but he was hoping to convince her to move closer to the ranch once they had Eli home safe. "Your decision, Wyn."

"I can't deal with talking to my father right now. He'll ask questions that I don't really want to answer." She stared down at her phone. "Maybe it's the coward's way out, but I'll send a resignation email."

"Are you sure?" He felt the need to give her an out. "We could be off base."

"I'm sure. We're not off base. And even if we are, I don't care what the reason is behind Eli's kidnapping." She glanced up at him. "I was planning to move again anyway. For sure I'm not staying on the rez after this."

He couldn't blame her for wanting to get away, although hearing that she had planned to move eventually was a surprise. As he approached the intersection, he hesitated before turning right to head straight north.

He needed to believe they were on the right track. That Eli and his kidnapper weren't that far ahead of them. But as he chugged up a hill, he was losing hope that they would find him.

"Chase! I think that's a car up ahead!" Wyn's hand gripped his arm. "Heading toward Pavillion!"

"I see it." He hit the gas. The engine growled in response as it pulled the trailer forward. "What kind of car is it?"

"I can't tell." She strained against the seatbelt, leaning forward as if that might help the SUV close the gap. "I don't know that much about cars."

"I meant the color mostly." Clouds were moving across the sky, obscuring the sun. He hoped they weren't an indication of an impending storm.

"All I can tell is that it's dark in color." She frowned. "Wait, I think he's slowing down to turn. He's not using his blinker, though."

"That's okay, we'll catch up to him." At least, he hoped they would. He pushed the SUV as fast as he dared. To the right, he could see a scattering of buildings, not bunched together but enough that he assumed the town of Pavillion was over there.

Interesting that the guy seemed to be heading left, away from town. Maybe there were other homes in that direction too.

His phone rang. Griff's name showed up on the screen, so he declined to answer. A few seconds later, the phone rang again.

Grinding his teeth, he answered, "I'm busy!"

"You were supposed to stay with the body!" Griff shot back. "Where are you?"

"A few miles outside of Pavillion." He glanced at Wyn. "If you don't hear from us in thirty minutes, you may want to head out to investigate."

Griff muttered something that may have been a curse. "I told you to stay out of this. To let us handle it."

"You wouldn't stay out if it was your son." He belatedly realized he'd never mentioned that fact to Griff. Although the tribal police officers seemed to already be aware of the biological connection.

"Your son?" Griff's voice rose in agitation. "You never mentioned that, Sullivan. Neither did Doug Bridges."

"It's a long story, and my family doesn't know." Wasn't that the understatement of the year? He needed to call Doug soon. "Besides, we haven't found anything significant. A dark car is several miles ahead of us, but the driver could be anyone."

There was a long silence. "I don't like this," Griff finally said. "If your dog alerts on anything out there, I want you to call me. Understand? Don't go chasing after your son without backup."

Picturing the dead George Twofeathers in the back of his truck made him swallow hard. He understood what Griff was saying. He could easily be outgunned. It was one thing to put himself in danger, but dragging Wyn and Rocky into harm's way wasn't good.

"Okay, I'll let you know if Rocky alerts on Eli's scent." Wyn's frown indicated she didn't like that response. "But when you're finished at the scene of the murder, you may want to head here. I don't think they'd take Eli to the Casino or Fort Washakie."

"And that's based on what? The sighting of one car?" Griff sounded weary and annoyed. "Stay in touch, Sullivan. I mean it."

"I will." He couldn't afford to alienate the FBI agent. Not just because of the kidnapping, but he and his siblings often worked with law enforcement across the state. He didn't want to prevent anyone from calling on their search and rescue services because he was at odds with the federal government. "Thanks, Griff. I'm sorry we didn't stick around."

"No, you're not," Griff shot back. "But now that I know Eli is your son, your actions make more sense. You should have told us that from the start."

To Chase's mind, it didn't matter who Eli's father was. "We all want the same thing. To find Eli alive and bring him home."

"Yes, we do. Later." Griff ended the call.

Chase quickly called Doug. His soon-to-be brother-in-law didn't answer, so he left a terse message. "We're tracking a car that may belong to Eli's kidnapper near the town of Pavillion. If you don't hear from me soon, you should contact the FBI."

There was a long pause as they drove in silence. Then Wyn spoke up. "Can't you go any faster? I think the dark car up ahead turned off this road. I don't see him anymore."

"I'm doing my best. We don't even know he's the kidnapper." Chase used his chin to gesture to the road before them and the intersection up ahead. "Is that where he turned?"

"Yes."

He swung the SUV into a wide turn. The roads out here were narrow, so he took up both lanes. After making the turn, he frowned. "Where did he go?"

"I don't know." Anxiety radiated off Wyn. "There are more hills out that way, so it's harder to see where the vehicle went. And it looks like there may be a few houses in the distance. Maybe the car has pulled off the road into one of those driveways?"

"It's possible." Chase tried to think of a way to narrow their search. He crested the top of a hill and saw the few homes she'd mentioned. He abruptly pulled off the road, as far as he could without getting stuck in the snow. "I think we need to use Rocky from this point forward."

"That's a good idea." Wyn looked relieved. "Your K9 has not steered us wrong yet."

"He's got a great nose." He shifted into park and killed the engine. "Remember the rules. We stay back and let him take the lead. And you need to stay behind me as we follow him. The kidnapper has already killed George Twofeathers." He shot her a grim look. "We know exactly what he's capable of."

"I will." Her face was pale. "I don't like knowing we're putting Rocky in danger, yet I'm not sure what else to do."

He nodded. Rocky's K9 vest was made of bullet-resistant material, but he also knew that dogs didn't do well with blunt-force trauma.

A bullet striking the K9 vest would cause internal bleeding. Considering they were in the middle of the Wind River

Reservation without quick access to emergency veterinary services, the risk to Rocky was significant.

As was the risk to Eli. A killer had their son.

He had little choice but to send Rocky out to find Eli's scent.

Pushing out of the car, he opened the back hatch. Rocky eagerly jumped down and lowered his head to stretch his back. He poured water into the collapsible bowl, and this time, Rocky lapped at it. Chase was under no illusions that Rocky was drinking on command. He knew the dog was likely thirsty.

"Are you ready?" He raised his voice to get Rocky revved up. "Are you ready to work?" Rocky's tail wagged back and forth in response. The K9 eagerly sniffed the air. He offered Rocky the scent bag with Eli's clothes. Rocky only gave it a passing sniff.

That was okay. Chase wasn't worried. He knew his dog had Eli's scent imprinted in his memory.

"Let's go search! Search for Eli!" Chase closed the back hatch and spread his arm wide. He waited as Rocky stood sniffing the air for several long seconds. Then the dog began his zigzag pattern of trying to capture Eli's scent.

Chase had his weapon in his coat pocket but decided against pulling it out at this point. The cold winter air would numb his fingers well before he'd have a chance to use the weapon.

He glanced back at Wyn. Their eyes met and held. He reached out, pulled her into his arms, and gave her a quick kiss. "Let's go."

She nodded but didn't say anything. He set off after Rocky, following the dog across the snowy terrain. The snow was packed down, which made the surface a little slippery. He glanced back at Wyn, hoping she wouldn't slip and fall.

Rocky was a dog on a mission. How his K9 could track elusive scents floating through the air was a mystery, but it soon became clear that Rocky had latched onto something.

"Good boy," Chase called out encouragingly. Not that Rocky really needed it. The dog's ears were pricked forward, and his nose was working a mile a minute.

The dog turned toward a ramshackle house off to his right. Chase's pulse kicked into high gear. Maybe they had been following the kidnapper's dark car. Quickening his pace to keep up with his dog, he scanned the property. Smoke rose from a chimney, indicating someone was home, but he didn't see a car.

There was an outbuilding a hundred yards away. That gave him pause. He didn't think there had been enough time for the kidnapper to park in the outbuilding, then walk to the house with Eli.

Yet it was clear Rocky was headed for the house.

When they were within fifty feet or so of the residence, Chase pulled off his glove and reached for his weapon. Even though they were close enough to be seen, nobody came out to confront them.

Rocky's nose was low to the ground again, and he veered to the left. Then his K9 stopped to sniff the ground for a moment. Rocky sat and let out a sharp bark.

He'd alerted on Eli's scent!

Chase ran forward, keeping a wary eye on the residence. When he got close to Rocky, he saw what had caught his K9's attention.

A small, black stuffed horse was lying on the ground. He turned as Wyn caught up to him. "Is that Eli's?"

"Yes. A gift from his grandfather." She bent to pick it up, then glanced at the house with apprehension. "Do you think Eli is inside?"

It was a good question. He needed to reward his dog, but their situation was precarious. Without warning, the sound of an engine roaring to life had him swinging toward the outbuilding.

A snowmobile shot out from the back of the structure, racing across the snowy terrain.

And there was no mistaking the shape of a small child perched in front of the driver.

14

Wyn gaped in horror as she watched the snow machine roar away from the property. Had that been Eli sitting in front of the driver? She turned toward Chase. He'd lobbed the red ball into the air for Rocky, but then turned to sprint toward the trailer.

Obviously, he was getting the snowmobiles. She took off after him, running clumsily in her snow boots. Rocky galloped alongside them with the red ball in his mouth, seemingly thrilled to have won the search game. While she was glad to know Eli had been there, her heart ached for her son. Eli would be at a loss without his stuffed horse, especially after losing his building block.

She could only pray that they'd catch up to him sooner than later.

Yet even as she slowed to a stop at the side of the trailer, she wondered where the kidnapper was taking him. Why had the kidnapper killed George, brought Eli way out here, only to take off again on the snow machine?

Chase had the trailer disconnected from the SUV. He'd pushed it back several feet and had lifted the cover. Seconds later, the first snow machine roared to life. He drove it off the trailer and onto the snow. Then he did the same with the second snow machine.

"Hand," he said sharply to Rocky.

Surprisingly, the dog dropped the ball into Chase's hand.

"Good boy." He rummaged in one of the bags. "Here, take this helmet and face mask. You'll have to keep up with me, understand?"

"I can do it." She donned the face mask first, then the helmet, tightening the strap under her chin. "I just need a quick lesson."

"I know." Chase tugged his face mask and helmet on, then gestured to the sled. "Jump on. It's relatively easy."

She straddled the seat.

"Here's the key." He turned it, and the engine roared to life. "You give the engine gas using the thumb button on the right handgrip. The brakes are just like those found on a bicycle. This is the switch for the hand warmers." He flipped it on. "They'll help battle the cold. And don't forget to lean into your turns. But be careful not to turn too sharply or you'll risk landing in the snow."

She tested his instructions. The sled surged forward when she used her thumb to give it gas. She used the brakes to make it stop. He was right, driving the machine wasn't too complicated.

"Rocky, search! Search for Eli!" Chase shouted the command loud enough to be heard over the sound of the engine.

She wasn't sure why he'd asked Rocky to search since they could simply follow the tracks in the snow, but she didn't waste time asking. This could be Chase's way of keeping his K9 engaged. Whatever worked was fine with her.

When Chase hit the gas, sending his sled forward, she quickly followed him across the snowy landscape toward the outbuilding. Under normal circumstances, flying across the snow like this would be exhilarating.

Instead, she felt sick, her stomach twisted into double knots. They were close on Eli's trail, but she instinctively knew this wouldn't be as easy as asking the kidnapper for her son back. This guy had taken him for a reason. In truth, she was scared to death to learn why Eli had been put in harm's way.

She pressed her thumb harder against the gas, increasing her speed to catch up with Chase. He was going fast, but not so much that he outpaced his K9. She was impressed with how Rocky moved through the snow, lifting his snout to the air and sniffing intently. She couldn't see anything beyond Chase's machine, but as they went deeper into the wilderness, she belatedly realized there were other snow machine tracks, going off in different directions.

What if they followed the wrong tracks? It had taken Chase at least ten minutes to get the sleds off the trailer.

Ten minutes of the kidnapper going anywhere from twenty to thirty miles per hour across the snow with their son. Moving him to yet another unknown destination.

Why? The word reverberated through her mind as she drove. They went from open fields to a wooded area. And when she narrowly missed a tree, she slowed her speed and focused on driving.

It was harder to keep track of Chase and Rocky once they entered the woods. She prayed the kidnapper wouldn't fall off his snowmobile with Eli. These things didn't have seat belts, and Eli hadn't been wearing a child-sized helmet.

When she turned around a cluster of trees, she saw Chase and Rocky weren't that far ahead. Chase had stopped his snow machine and was examining the ground. She gunned the engine to catch up.

"What's wrong?" No point in trying to keep her voice down, the engine noise would alert Eli's kidnapper that they were closing in.

"Lots of snow machine tracks here." He turned to Rocky. "Search for Eli!"

Rocky stood and sniffed the air for a few long moments. Then the dog turned left on the trail, sniffing at some brush along the way. He stopped near some slender tree branches that were about waist high. Then Rocky sat and let out a sharp bark.

His alert! She rose to a standing position with her booted feet on either side of the sled seat. "What is it? What did Rocky find?"

"I don't see anything obvious." Chase had gotten off the sled and was examining the ground. Then he seemed to notice the same thing she did. The way Rocky's nose was practically touching the tree branch. "Is that what you smell?" Chase asked with a frown. "Are you telling me Eli came through this way?"

Rocky gave another sharp bark and continued to stare up at Chase as if willing him to read the dog's mind. Chase glanced at her, shrugged, and climbed back up on his sled. Then he rummaged in a duffel clipped to the back of the seat. He filled a collapsible bowl with water and set it on the ground for the dog. Rocky slurped the water eagerly, obviously needing a break. When Rocky finished, Chase put the bowl away and turned to face her.

"I'm not sure why he alerted on those branches. But I

trust Rocky. His nose has not failed me yet." He raised his voice. "Good boy! Search! Search for Eli!"

Rocky jumped up from his sitting position to bound along the left-hand trail, following some invisible scent only he could identify. The dog was excited to play this game, which was a good thing.

Chase gunned the engine of his sled to follow, so she did too.

Navigating the snowmobile through the woods was harder than she'd anticipated. Not just because they often had to take unexpected turns, forcing her to use all her upper-arm strength to get the skis to shift directions. But also because she had to keep the tips of her skis from being snagged on trees and bushes.

While staying focused on the trail ahead of her, low-hanging branches slapped her in the face. She wondered if that's what had happened to Eli. It would explain why Rocky had alerted on her son's scent back there.

She tried to see it as a positive thing that they were on the right track. Yet as they threaded their snowmobiles through the woods, she couldn't help but worry about what they'd find when they reached the end of the trail. They'd made it this far; she couldn't bear to find Eli just in time for the kidnappers to harm him in some way.

She swallowed hard against the seemingly endless panic. She needed to remain calm. To stay positive. To trust in God's plan.

And to pray.

Please, Lord Jesus, keep Eli safe in Your care!

∾

LOUD. Eli wanted to cover his ears with his hands. The machine they were riding was too loud.

But that wasn't the worst thing. He was sad he'd lost his stuffy. It was all Scary Man's fault. He'd fallen asleep in the truck and woke up when the scary man grabbed him. He'd had his stuffy in his hand as the scary man carried him outside. Then the scary man yelled something, startling him. Eli realized that's when he must have dropped it. He'd wanted to use his words to tell Scary Man to go back and look for it, but there wasn't time when the scary man turned to go inside and started working on the loud machine.

Then Scary Man plopped him on the seat of the loud machine, and they were moving outside and across the open snow.

He still had the hard thing in his other hand. He'd managed to get the small cylinder into his palm under his mittens. He was glad to have the hard thing cupped in his hand, but he also felt off balance again.

He squeezed his hand.

Hard. Hard. Hard.

He tried to rock, but the scary man yelled at him to knock it off. Eli wondered if his rocking might cause them to fall off the loud machine, so he'd stopped and sat as still as possible. The scary man was holding him tightly across his tummy, which made him feel a little safe.

His nose was running across his face. He swiped at his cheek with his sleeve as the branches scraped past. They had been out in the open, but now they were in the woods. He couldn't tell where they were going. And it wasn't easy to concentrate without his stuffy. He opened and closed his empty hand, wishing he had the stuffed horsey. Then he closed his fingers around the short, hard thing. That helped. He liked holding something in his hand.

The movement of the loud machine also made him feel a little better. The rocking was more side to side than back and forth, but that was okay. He didn't mind the machine carrying them across the snow. If it wasn't so loud, and if he wasn't with Scary Man, he might have had fun.

But he was tired of being with Scary Man. Smelly Man had been nice to him, but Scary Man yelled a lot. He wanted to go home. He knew his mommy was coming for him. Every time he'd started to cry, he could see his mommy's face smiling down at him and telling him not to worry. She loved him and would be there soon.

So he hadn't cried. Or yelled. Or let the scary man know how upset he was. He stayed quiet because that was his superpower.

And he hoped his mommy was waiting at the place where the scary man was taking him.

CHASE COULDN'T SEE much beyond the trees. He didn't like knowing that by taking the snowmobiles, they were announcing their arrival for everyone to hear. He'd much rather sneak up on the kidnapper, but that ship had sailed.

He slowed his speed to keep pace with Rocky. From what he could tell, Rocky was doing okay. The K9 had incredible stamina. Still, he kept a wary eye on his partner. If it looked as if Rocky was getting tired, he could always carry the dog in front of him on the sled. The only way to keep Rocky safe was to have the dog facing him with his front legs draped over Chase's shoulders.

Rocky wasn't a fan of that method of traveling, but he'd cooperate. Yet Chase was hoping that wouldn't be necessary.

Their short break seemed to have rejuvenated the K9's desire to find Eli.

Chase hadn't rewarded Rocky for alerting on the bushes because the game wasn't over. Those in-between alerts were hard to manage sometimes. Watching the way Rocky darted between the trees, he'd decided it was better he hadn't taken the time to reward the K9.

After he turned around a large pine tree, he saw the dark building in the distance. He released the gas and clamped on the brakes, coming to a stop. "Rocky, heel!"

The dog slowed to a stop, glanced back at him as if to ask why. He killed the engine on the snowmobile, and that was enough for Rocky to turn and trot back to them.

Wynona brought her snowmobile to a stop behind him. "What is it?"

He gestured to the dark-brown cabin located almost two hundred yards away. "I think that might be our destination."

Wyn's eyes were wide behind her helmet. "What are you going to do?"

That was a good question. Chase eyed the cabin, trying to figure out a way to approach without being seen. It's not as if the occupants probably hadn't heard the snow machines. They weren't quiet. The tracks of the sled that had taken Eli from the last house cut directly across the open land. There were trees behind the cabin, so maybe he could go around.

Rocky stood beside the snow machine patiently waiting.

After a long minute, he took off his helmet and turned to face Wyn. She removed her helmet, too, so they could communicate better. "I need you to call Griff to let him know where we are. And wait here for him to get here. I'm going to head through the woods on foot with Rocky to approach the house from the back."

"I'm coming with you."

He narrowed his gaze. "Wyn, I need you to call for backup. Do you have any idea where we are? Because I don't."

"Not really." She jumped off the snowmobile. "We can call Griff, but there's no reason to sit here to wait. Griff and the tribal police don't have snow machines."

He had to admit she was right about that. It was unlikely that Griff and the tribal police would get here in time to be of any help.

Still, he needed to try. Maybe once he found a way inside the cabin, he could stall long enough for help to arrive.

He pulled out his phone and stared at his screen. One lousy bar.

He should have anticipated there wouldn't be good cell service out here. Rather than calling, he sent a text. In his experience, text messages often got through even with limited service.

Then he dismounted from his sled and gestured to the woods. "Let's head this way. The goal is to stay hidden within the trees as long as possible."

"I understand." Her tone was subdued. "Griff and the police are not going to get here in time, are they?"

"They might." He grimaced, knowing that was a lie. He wished he'd asked Doug Bridges, Maya, and his other siblings to come to the reservation earlier. Now it was too late. He'd left Doug a message but knew they were hours away by car.

Unfortunately, they were on their own. And Wyn deserved to know the truth. "Probably not. That's why I wanted you to stay back here. If I get into trouble, you can take the sled back to the SUV and drive out to meet with Griff from there."

"I can't leave, Chase." Her brown eyes pleaded with his. "Don't ask me to. Eli is probably scared and confused. He won't understand what's going on. And I'm worried about how he'll react to another stranger taking him away."

He wouldn't be a stranger to his own son if she hadn't kept her pregnancy a secret. But there was no point in rehashing the past. He forced himself to nod in agreement.

"Try to stay behind me in case they start shooting." He winced, and quickly added, "I just want you to be safe. I'm sure we'll figure something out once we get there."

"We will." She didn't sound confident, and that only made him feel worse. As they stayed within the shelter of the trees, he tried to think of a way to get additional support. He pulled out his phone again, took off his gloves, and texted Doug as a follow-up to his earlier message. He kept it short.

We're heading to a cabin ten miles outside Pavillion to rescue Eli. If you don't hear from me in an hour, send a search team.

Since he needed to make sure his hands were free to pull his weapon if needed, he dropped the phone into his coat pocket without waiting for a reply. Knowing Doug, his soon-to-be brother-in-law would likely hit the road the minute he received Chase's text, which wasn't a bad thing.

His plan was simple. Do everything in his power to keep Eli and Wyn alive long enough for Doug, his siblings, or Griff and the tribal police to get there.

He kept an eye on his K9 as they walked through the trees. Rocky seemed fine; he didn't hold up his paws in a way that indicated the pads were sore. He should have brought the booties along, even though Rocky hated them and did everything he could to get them off.

Between Rocky, Wyn, and Eli, he battled a sense of failure. He should have waited for Griff to get there before taking off on the snowmobiles to follow Eli. Maybe they could have approached the cabin from another direction.

Although without Rocky's alerting along the way, they wouldn't even be this close to Eli. So he swallowed his fear of failing and pressed on.

A solid fifteen minutes passed in silence. Then the trees thinned, and he realized they'd reached the end of the woods.

They'd gotten at least a hundred yards closer to the cabin. From there, he could see the snow machine parked off to the side as well as smoke rising from the chimney. A sense of unease snaked down his spine.

It almost seemed as if the cabin owners were waiting, anticipating their arrival.

A trap? He glanced at Wyn, who stared at the cabin with a hint of fear, desperation, and resolve.

Rocky sniffed the air. Chase hadn't told him to search, but the way Rocky's nose was going, he knew his K9 would dart straight toward the snowmobile to alert on Eli's scent.

"Easy, boy," he murmured. Then he turned to look at Wyn. "Stay back just long enough for me to reach the side of the house. If anyone starts shooting, you turn back and get to the sleds."

She didn't want to, but she reluctantly nodded. "If they don't start shooting, I'll run over to join you."

"Okay." He debated leaving Rocky behind with Wyn, then decided it was better to keep him. Wyn was a rookie on the snowmobile, she wouldn't be able to ride back with Rocky sharing her seat. Plus, Rocky only listened to him when he felt like it. No way would his K9 take orders from Wyn.

He drew in a deep breath and let it out slowly. This was

it. He gave Wyn a quick kiss, then darted across the clearing. "Come, Rocky," he called softly.

His K9 eagerly followed.

Chase half expected the front door to bang open and for bullets to fly. But there was no sound other than his breathing and his footsteps crunching on the snow as he ran.

When he reached the side of the building, he edged toward the window. It was covered by a curtain, making it impossible to see inside. He forced thoughts of Eli being locked in the room or tied to a chair out of his mind as he continued along the side of the cabin until he could peer around the corner toward the front door.

Still nothing.

That didn't make sense. He knew the snowmobiles must have been heard by the kidnapper. Rocky stayed close as if sensing the threat.

He glanced over his shoulder in time to see Wyn making her move. When she broke from the protection of the trees and ran toward him, he quickly turned to watch the front door, anticipating a reaction from the kidnapper.

Nobody came outside.

A chill that had nothing to do with the cold temperature slid down his spine. What in the world was going on here? Was it possible they'd mistakenly followed the wrong trail? Had he imagined the smaller figure of a child on the snow machine?

No, Rocky had alerted to Eli's scent. He was convinced Eli was inside the house. Rocky nudged him, as if silently agreeing.

"What's wrong?" Wyn's voice was a whisper.

"Not sure." They needed to do something to catch the

kidnappers off guard. "Let's go around to the back side of the house."

"Right behind you," she agreed.

He quickly crossed to the opposite corner. Rocky stayed close, as did Wyn. When he peeked out, he didn't see anyone outside with a gun. He stepped forward, edging along the side of the cabin. He almost wished there was a major snow-storm or something that would help hide their presence.

There was nothing but the whistling wind.

Chase made it all the way to the back door when it abruptly opened, and a tall, thin, dark-skinned man stepped out with a gun. "It's about time. We've been waiting."

Chase froze. This was a trap. He abruptly realized that if this guy intended to shoot them outright, they'd already be dead. He didn't glance at his dog, too afraid to call attention to his K9 partner. "We've come for Eli."

"This way." The tall Native American stepped back, the gun still leveled at Chase's chest. "As I said. We've been waiting."

Every one of his instincts was on high alert, but Chase knew they had no choice but to come inside. He crossed the threshold first. Rocky followed along with Wyn.

"Don't be stupid," the tall, thin man said. "If you try anything, your son will suffer."

His son. The words hit hard. Chase didn't know this man, but it almost seemed as if the Native American knew him.

"What do you want from us?" Wyn asked, speaking for the first time. "Is this about the audit I was doing for the tribal leaders? If so, you should know I quit my job. I'm no longer employed by the council. In fact, once I have Eli back safe, I'll be leaving the reservation, forever."

There was a long silence. With this man holding them at gunpoint, their chances of getting out of this alive were slim.

But he wouldn't give up hope.

A quick glance around the living area didn't reveal any sign of Eli. Then he noticed Rocky had disappeared too. Had the dog slipped past the kidnappers to find their son? Maybe. He found himself hoping the big dog didn't scare the little boy.

Either way, not finding Eli safe and unharmed was sending Wyn over the edge.

More than she already was.

"What do you want?" Wyn abruptly shouted. "Tell me! I don't even know you! If this isn't about the audit, then why did you kidnap my son?"

"A child for a child," a flat female voice said.

Chase turned to see who had spoken. A woman stepped from the shadows. She, too, held a gun.

Her gaze locked with his. The woman standing before him was thin and gaunt, her long dark hair now streaked with gray, but despite those differences in her appearance, he instantly recognized her.

Tonya Redstone.

Alecia's mother.

And the way she was pointing the gun at him, eyeing him with frank hatred, Chase understood that this was about him. About Tonya wanting to kill him for failing to find her daughter alive.

15

A *child for a child?* Wynona stared at the angry young woman pointing her gun at them. Her words sent a wave of sickening dread washing over her.

Would this woman ruthlessly murder a child?

"Tonya, I'm very sorry about Alecia," Chase said calmly. "I understand why you blame me for not finding her sooner." He took a step toward her, lifting his hands palms forward. "You should kill me, not Eli. He doesn't deserve to die."

Chase's offer to die in place of their son made Wyn's breath hitch in her chest. She knew he wasn't bluffing. She knew he would absolutely die to protect Eli.

And to protect her too. He was an amazing man whom she'd hurt very badly. And if they got out of this . . .

No, *when* they got out of this, she would do her best to make amends.

"You should have found her," Tonya Redstone repeated. "You with your fancy equipment and your dog. Why didn't you find her?"

"Tonya, I'm sorry," Chase said. "Please know I would have done anything to bring Alecia back home safe. Her death has haunted me for months. I wish Rocky and I could have gotten there sooner. But Eli doesn't deserve your anger and revenge. Please, let him and his mother go. They're not responsible for what happened to Alecia."

"Ah, but Eli is your son." A glitter of anger sparked in Tonya's dark eyes. "I think it would be fitting for you to watch your son die, the way I had to find my dead daughter."

Wyn frowned, wondering how Tonya knew that Eli was Chase's son. Then it hit her. Redstone. Her father served on the tribal council with Hank Redstone. Hank was too old to be Tonya's husband. But maybe her father?

Wyn's father must have mentioned how Chase was Eli's father. Although she was at a loss as to why he would do such a thing. She had to assume that Chase's name had come up by coincidence. Her father couldn't have known anything about what the Redstone family would do with that information.

Unless—no way. Her father doted on Eli. And she wished she'd spoken to her father in person rather than sending the email.

Not that it mattered now. There was no help coming anytime soon. She and Chase were alone. And they needed to figure out a way to convince Tonya Redstone not to follow through on her plan.

"Please," Wyn said, speaking up for the first time. "Please let Eli go. He's a little boy who doesn't deserve this."

The woman's gaze darted toward her. "Are you saying my Alecia deserved to die?"

"No, of course not." Wyn tried to think of a way to reach

through this woman's grief and anger. "I would be just as upset as you are if something happened to Eli. It's our job to protect our children." She heard the low rumble an engine coming from somewhere outside and hoped this woman didn't have reinforcements on the way. "But you must know that killing Eli won't bring Alecia back."

"A child for a child!" Tonya practically spat the words. "I will feel better when I know that you have suffered as much as I have!"

"We've been suffering during the time you've taken Eli away from us," Chase said. "You've had Eli much longer than I searched for Alecia." He lowered his hands, tucking them into his pockets. "If you want revenge, take me. Kill me." He glanced around the cabin. "I'll go outside with you right now. We can end this once and for all."

Wyn noticed that Alecia Redstone's mother looked a bit uncertain by Chase's offer to head outside. Maybe the woman had underestimated her ability to take another person's life. The last thing Wyn wanted was to lose Chase or Eli, but she felt powerless to prevent it.

But she had to try. "If you do this, you may never be aligned with Alecia in the spirit world." Wyn fell back on some of her early stories from her father's family. The Native Americans didn't believe in God or Christianity the way Chase had taught her, but they did believe in an afterlife of sorts. "What is Alecia's spirit animal? Has your daughter been back to visit you?"

"She was too young to have identified with a spirit animal." Then Alecia's mother looked uncertain. "I have seen a goldfinch flying near our home very often in the past few months." Her voice dropped. "Yellow was Alecia's favorite color."

"So you have seen Alecia's spirit animal," Wyn said softly. "Your daughter has identified with the goldfinch. I think Alecia wants you to know she's okay, that she loves flying across the sky. And that she's waiting for you to join her in the spirit world."

The tip of Tonya's gun lowered a bit as she considered Wyn's words. "Do you really think the goldfinch is Alecia's spirit animal?"

"Yes, I do," Wyn said. "She is waiting for you, Tonya. She wants to be reunited with you in the spirit world very soon."

Chase moved beside her, and suddenly she understood his plan.

She wanted to cry out a protest, but it was too late. Several things happened at once. Chase darted forward while pulling his gun from his pocket. Tonya pulled the trigger, and her gun went off seconds before Chase disarmed her.

Expecting the man behind them to start shooting, too, Wyn dropped to a crouch as the door of the cabin burst open. A tall man with brown hair rushed inside. She lashed out at the young Native American with her foot, catching his knee. The man howled but didn't get a chance to fire his weapon as the newcomer knocked the weapon from his hands.

Wyn wanted to bow her head in gratitude, but Eli's well-being was all that mattered. She glanced at Chase to make sure he hadn't been hit but Tonya's bullet. "Eli?" She darted behind Tonya to the rooms behind her. "Eli? I'm here! Mommy's here!"

"Mommy!" Eli's voice sounded hoarse as he called out to her. She barged into the bedroom and found him on the bed with Rocky stretched out beside him. Eli's right hand grasped a handful of the dog's fur. "Mommy!"

"I'm here, Eli. I'm here." She sank down on the other side of her son and gathered him close. Eli rested his forehead against her.

"I knew you'd come," he said.

"Always." Tears filled her eyes, and she hugged him hard. Rocky's dark eyes watched them. She was grateful the dog had come inside to sit by her son, keeping him company as they faced his kidnappers.

Their nightmare was over. For the first time in almost twenty-four hours, the panic that plagued her faded away.

Eli was safe.

SOFT. Hard. Soft. Hard.

Eli hadn't been afraid of the big doggy. The doggy had put his head on Eli's lap, and when Eli felt his soft fur, he was back in balance again.

Soft. Hard. Soft. Hard.

He'd thought he'd heard his mommy's voice in the other room, but the scary man had told him to stay there and to keep quiet, so he hadn't gotten off the bed to look. Then the big doggy had come in, and Eli had felt safe. The loud bang had scared him, but the doggy stayed right next to him.

He squeezed the doggy's fur. Soft. Hard. Soft. Hard.

He had known his mommy would come to find him. It had taken a long time, but that was okay. She was here now.

"What's that in your hand?" his mom asked.

He sat up and looked from the soft doggy to his mom. Then he opened his clenched left hand to show her the small, hard thing.

"Eli, where did you get that?" His mom sounded upset.

He shrugged. But when she stared at him, he knew she wanted him to use his words. "In the back seat of the car."

When she tried to take it, he quickly closed his fingers around it. "Hard. Soft. Hard. Soft," he whispered.

"Okay, I understand." His mother glanced up at the doorway. "We found your wooden building block, but we gave it to the police. We'll get you another building block when we get home, okay? I have your horsey here. Do you want it?"

He nodded and leaned against her again. The doggy stayed at his side.

Soft. Hard.

He was happy to know he'd be going home soon.

CHASE COULDN'T BELIEVE Doug Bridges had shown up at the cabin. And even more so to learn his sister Jessica had chartered a plane piloted by her old high school friend Logan Fletcher to bring Doug to the rez.

"How did you find us?" he asked, after he'd bound Tonya Redstone's wrists behind her back as Doug did the same thing with the young man whom he was pretty sure had killed George Twofeathers.

"Jess tracked your snowmobiles." Doug grinned. "Your family takes safety measures to an extreme, but in this case, that paranoia has worked out well. We were already in the air when your message came through. That helped us refine our search area."

"That's amazing." Chase knew some of that paranoia was related to the way they'd lost their parents. He'd forgotten about the AirTag trackers they'd put in their snowmobiles years ago. "Thanks for coming."

"Hey, I had to convince Jess to let me ride along," Doug said, shaking his head. "She would have come by herself, even though she wasn't armed."

That made Chase scowl. He saw Jessica hovering in the doorway of the cabin, her large Belgian sheepdog, Teddy, at her side. Behind her stood Logan. Chase gave his sister an exasperated look. "Jess, you're not a cop."

"I know that." She shrugged, resting her hand on Teddy's head. "I let Doug come, didn't I?" She glanced over her shoulder at Logan. "I should say Logan insisted Doug tag along."

Chase was surprised Maya hadn't insisted on coming too. Logan's plane was relatively small, though, and adding another person may have been too much. He sighed and smiled grimly. "Well, thanks. Your timing was perfect."

"What's this about you having a son?" Jess asked.

Doug winced. "I thought you were going to wait to bring that up." To Chase, he added, "I spoke to Griff on the way here."

Chase sighed again, knowing this conversation was inevitable. He hadn't met his own son yet for himself, but hearing movement in the doorway, he turned to find Wynona carrying Eli into the living area.

Their son looked more like his mother in person, but there were a few hints of Chase's DNA. Especially in the boy's chin and his ears. Chase wanted to rush forward but knew that trying to embrace the little boy would scare Eli.

"Eli, this is Chase." Wyn's voice was low. "He and Rocky are a search and rescue team. They helped me find you."

Eli lifted his head to look down at Rocky. He frowned, then looked at Chase. "Soft. Not hard like a rock. Soft."

Chase smiled, his throat thick with emotion. "Yes, I

know. Rocky's fur is very soft. But he has a hard head when it comes to doing what he wants."

Eli nodded solemnly. "Soft and hard."

"Exactly." He blinked tears from his eyes and cleared his throat. "It's nice to meet you, Eli."

Eli didn't say anything in response to that. Chase didn't mind. Just seeing his son alive and unharmed was enough for now.

"Eli found something in the car," Wyn said. "Can you show them, Eli?" His son slowly opened his hand revealing a bullet. Chase stared at Wynona who shrugged. "What can I say? Eli likes contrasts."

"I see." He glanced over to where Doug stood frowning over the man he'd disarmed. "I have a feeling we're going to need that as evidence. To match it with the bullet used to, uh"—he caught himself in the nick of time—"to take care of George Twofeathers."

"Yes, I thought so." Wyn flashed him a grateful look. "I gave Eli his stuffed horsey. If he could get his building block back, he'd be thrilled."

"We'll get your building blocks very soon," Chase told the little boy.

Eli nodded. "Thank you."

Again, Chase felt his eyes tear up. "You're welcome."

"I have something hard," Logan said, entering the room behind Jess. He held up a small stone arrowhead. "Would you like this, Eli?"

Eli leaned forward to see the arrowhead, then nodded. And just like that, Eli had swapped the bullet for the stone arrowhead. "Hard," Eli whispered. He lifted the stone arrow and the stuffed horse. "Soft and hard."

Chase gave Logan a nod of appreciation. Logan simply shrugged.

Picking up on Eli's unique personality, Jess thankfully didn't ask any more questions about the fact that the boy was Chase's son. But she did glare at Wynona, likely upset about how Wyn had kept Eli a secret.

Ironically, Chase's anger had dissipated. There was no point in being upset about what he'd missed or what had been done in the past.

All that mattered was moving forward from here.

"You'll be glad to know Griff is on his way," Doug said, interrupting his thoughts.

"How do you know that?" Chase asked. "The cell service out here is nonexistent."

"As I mentioned, we spoke via radio while on the plane and asked him to meet us here." Doug waved a hand. "Don't you hear the sound of car engines?"

Now that Doug mentioned it, he did. Thank goodness, the feds were on their way. Chase narrowed his gaze on the gunman. "Who are you?"

The young man ignored him.

"Scary Man," Eli said.

Chase swung around to face Eli. "Did he hurt you?"

"No." Eli snuggled closer to his mother. "He wore the scary black mask."

That information was only slightly reassuring. Chase met Wynona's worried gaze and understood her concern. Eli didn't look as if he'd been hurt in any way, but they wouldn't know the full extent of the emotional impact to the little boy for some time yet. Considering his son's diagnosis, they may never understand what he'd suffered.

And that hurt. A lot.

"FBI!" Hearing Griff's shout, Chase turned to watch the agent enter the room with his gun in a two-handed grip. Griff's gaze swept over the two perps Chase had tied up before he lowered his weapon. "Looks like you don't need me."

"Trust me, we do." Chase gestured toward Tonya who sat expressionless, her gaze on the floor. "This is Tonya Redstone. She's Alecia Redstone's mother and blames me for her daughter's death."

"She confessed to kidnapping Eli," Wyn added. "Her goal was to make Chase suffer as much as she did. She threatened to kill Eli in retaliation for his not finding Alecia."

"Who's this?" Griff asked, gesturing to the gunman.

"He's not talking," Doug said with a shrug.

"He may have taken George Twofeathers out of the picture." Chase spoke carefully, aware that Eli was listening. Chase stepped forward to hand over the bullet. "Eli found this in the back of his car."

"Good. This should help us with a ballistics match." Griff's tone rang with satisfaction. "Okay, I'll need all your statements before we haul them into custody."

As if on cue, the tribal police filed into the room. From the way the two officers looked at Tonya Redstone and her accomplice, Chase could tell they were upset that two of their own were responsible for this.

"This man is Joshua Redstone," one of the officers said. "He is Tonya's cousin. They are both grandchildren of tribal leader Hank Redstone."

Chase glanced at Wyn who nodded. He realized that her father had played a role in Eli's kidnapping. Not on purpose, but a role nonetheless.

"Are you related to Julia Stone or Carl Longfoot?" Chase asked.

Tonya looked away, a flash of guilt in her eyes. It made him wonder if she'd used the name Julia Stone as an alias.

Wyn took Eli back to the bedroom to keep him from being overwhelmed by strangers. Surprisingly, Rocky had seemed to nominate himself as Eli's protector. His K9 followed them and stretched out beside the child. Eli gave up his stuffed horsey to bury his fingers in the dog's soft pelt.

After making sure Eli was okay, Chase filled Griff and Doug in on everything that had transpired. Doug took over the story about how he and Jess had hired Logan to fly them to the location of the snowmobiles' GPS trackers.

Griff took notes, as did the tribal police officers. Chase could tell that Griff would be taking over the case, in large part because these two perps were grandchildren of one of the Wind River tribal leaders.

When asked about the audit, both Joshua and Tonya looked confused. Chase had to admit that this kidnapping had been fueled by rage and revenge.

Not greed, the way he and Wynona had assumed.

Honestly, he wasn't sure which was worse. He'd felt guilty over his inability to save Alecia, but he hadn't killed her.

Not the way Tonya had intended to kill Eli.

Yet he also felt sorry for the grieving mother. To be consumed by her daughter's death to the point she would do something this drastic. This terrible.

He glanced at Eli and knew his faith would have gotten him through the loss. Not that it would have been easy. Losing a child could never be easy.

But he didn't think he'd seek revenge the way Tonya had.

"Are we able to leave now?" Wyn's weary eyes clung to his. "Eli wants to go home."

He wanted that, too, but his home was the Sullivan K9 Search and Rescue Ranch. And in that moment, he realized he couldn't simply pick Eli and Wyn up and move them from the rez directly to his cabin. The way he wanted to.

At least not yet. Eli needed time to recuperate. And Wynona did too.

"Yes, of course." He frowned. "We'll need to take the snow machines back to the SUV."

"I told Eli we'd have to ride them back," Wyn said. "He won't mind."

"Okay then." He managed a reassuring smile. "Let's go."

The trip back to the SUV on the sled was slow. Wyn had wanted Eli to ride with her, but in the end, he held the boy on his lap with one arm, driving the sled with the other. It wasn't easy, but they made it. Rocky galloped alongside, as if helping to keep an eye on Eli.

Wyn sat in the back seat of the SUV holding Eli as he made the long trip back to Riverton hauling the snowmobile trailer. In hindsight, he was extremely grateful he'd brought them along. It didn't take long for Eli to fall asleep.

"I don't know how to thank you," Wyn whispered. "You and Rocky were amazing."

He was a little surprised by her gratitude. "You don't blame me? Tonya kidnapped Eli because of me. Because in her mind, I killed her daughter."

Wyn met his gaze in the rearview mirror. "I'm the one to blame. If I hadn't kept Eli a secret . . ."

He sighed. Maybe it was the events of the day, but he was too tired to be angry anymore. "We both made mistakes, Wyn."

"Yes, but my mistakes were far worse." She looked away. "I hope you can forgive me."

He was touched by her confession. "I don't blame you. And I hope you can forgive me too."

"You were going to sacrifice yourself for Eli," she said, "the son you never met."

He shrugged. "Yeah, but my goal was to disarm her. I had hoped to get her outside so that you and Eli weren't in the line of fire. When I heard the plane, I knew help was on the way, so I decided to make my move then."

"I didn't realize the engine was from a plane." She looked down at her sleeping son. "I would have given my life for his too. But I'm glad we didn't have to."

"I agree." There was so much to discuss, but he figured they could do that later. Eli woke from his nap, rubbing his eyes, then searched for his toys—the stuffed horsey and the stone arrowhead.

"I'm hungry," Eli said softly.

"What would you like for dinner?" They had reached Riverton now, so he pulled up to the same fast-food restaurant where Eli had been earlier that day. "They have chicken fingers."

"Yes, please," Eli said. Then he hid his face against his mother.

Chase wished the little boy wasn't afraid of him. He ordered their meals, then headed for Wynona's house. He gave her the food so that he could get Rocky out of the back and grab his K9's dog food and dishes.

When Rocky had done his business and had spent a few minutes playing with his red ball as a late reward for finding Eli, they joined Wynona and Eli inside.

"We've been waiting for you." Wyn gestured toward the empty seat at the table.

He quickly dished out food for Rocky and gestured for his K9 to go ahead and eat. Then he sat on the other side of Eli. "Thank you for that. I'd like to say grace."

Wyn nodded and bowed her head. Eli didn't speak. He

understood now why Wyn had told the little boy that being silent was his superpower. He'd never been around a quieter child.

"Dear Lord Jesus, we thank You for this food and more importantly for guiding us to Eli. Thank You for keeping our son safe in Your loving arms. Amen."

"Amen," Wynona echoed.

Eli didn't say anything. Wyn tried to prod him. Chase shook his head. "It's okay."

"Eli needs to remember to use his words," Wyn said. "Right, Eli?"

"Right." Eli agreed. He looked down at Rocky who'd stretched out on the floor beside him and smiled. Then he took a bite of his chicken fingers smothered in ketchup.

Chase was almost jealous of the relationship Rocky had forged with his son.

It was only after Wynona put Eli to bed that they had time to talk. He took Rocky out one last time. The dog stretched out on the floor at his feet. He sank down onto the sofa and patted the cushion beside him. "Join me?"

"Of course." She did so, then surprised him by turning to hug him. "This was the longest day of my life."

He gathered her close. "For me too." He pressed a kiss to her temple. "Wyn, I still care about you. I'd like time to get to know Eli, of course, but I also want to spend time with you."

"I can't believe you're being so nice to me," she said, her voice muffled against his chest. "I wanted you to come back so badly, and when you didn't, I let my pride stand in the way of telling you about Eli."

"Wait, what?" He eased her upright so he could look into her eyes. "I did come back. Maybe not as quickly as I should have, but once things were settled with the family, I came back for you. But you were gone."

She looked confused, then realization dawned. "That must have been when I left to move in with my aunt. She was dying, and I promised my father I would help care for her."

Her father. He had to bite back his feelings for the man. He was about to tell her how her father had refused his request to marry her when there was a sharp knock on the door.

Wyn broke away and rose to answer it. Chase rose to his feet when he saw her father, Ogima Blackhorse, enter the room. The old man's eyes narrowed when he saw Chase.

"Why didn't you tell me about Eli being kidnapped?" her father demanded.

"Why did you tell Hank Redstone that Chase was Eli's father?" Wyn shot back. "That's how Alecia's mother knew to take Eli in the first place!"

"Easy, you'll wake Eli." Chase took a step closer until he was standing beside Wyn. The last missing puzzle piece fell into place. "You told Hank Redstone the truth on purpose, didn't you? Because you knew the Redstones held me responsible for Alecia's death."

Ogima's face flushed red. "Of course not."

But the truth was written there for everyone to see. Even Wyn.

"You should have given me permission to marry Wynona when I asked over five years ago," Chase continued. "If you had, Eli would never have been in any danger."

Now the color drained from the old man's face.

"What? You refused Chase's request? I can't believe it." Wyn's voice was choked with tears. "You knew I loved Chase. Why would you do that?"

"He's not good enough . . . ," her father started, but Wyn stepped back and held up a hand.

"Stop. I don't want to hear it." She straightened and stared her father down. "I love you, but I can't look at you right now. You almost lost your grandson today. And me. Your own daughter. Tonya Redstone was going to kill us all!"

"I didn't know Tonya was that far gone." Ogima's voice was apologetic. "I never would have put you and Eli in harm's way."

"But you did," Chase said. "Thankfully, we were able to escape with help from my family. Not yours. For now, I think Wynona needs time and space to come to grips with your role in this."

For the first time ever, Ogima backed down. He looked as if he wanted to say something, but turned away. His shoulders slumped in defeat as he left, closing the door softly behind him.

"I can't believe he did that," Wyn whispered. Then she turned and threw herself into Chase's arms. "You wanted to marry me?"

"Yes." He held her close. "I love you, Wyn. I always have. I never got over you."

"I love you too, Chase. So much." She lifted up on her tiptoes and kissed him. A real kiss. And just like five and a half years ago, when they'd allowed their passion to over-rule their common sense and willpower, heat instantly flared between them.

"Will you give me a second chance?" Chase pulled himself away from kissing her with an effort. "Will you and Eli come stay with me on the ranch for a while?"

"Yes. I'd like that. I want Eli to know you're his father." She kissed him again, then held his gaze. "And somehow, we'll have to find a way to forgive my father."

He forced himself to nod. "I don't want to be at odds with your father, Wyn. Eli needs his grandfather to show him the Native American way."

"I love you so much," she said again. "That's the nicest, sweetest thing you could ever have done for me."

"For us," he corrected. "For our family."

"For our family," she agreed.

Rocky nudged his side, as if putting his stamp of approval on their love too.

EPILOGUE

Four weeks later...

Wyn tried not to express her apprehension as Eli sat perched on the back of a dark golden-bay gelding named Scout. Chase stood beside the horse, his hand on his son's back, as Scout ambled slowly across the corral.

In the weeks they'd been on the ranch, Eli had opened up a bit. Oh, their son would never be a chatty Cathy, but he was doing better at using his words.

She personally thought Rocky was a big part of the reason. Eli loved that dog, and the two could always be found snuggled together on the sofa. Chase had noticed that, too, and had thought that Eli might do better with communicating with animals than with people.

Hence his first horseback riding lesson.

Eli didn't look at all scared to be up on Scout. One hand was wrapped in the horse's soft mane, and the other clutched the pommel of the saddle.

She could almost hear her son whispering, "Soft and hard."

They'd explained that Chase was his daddy, and Eli seemed to accept the news in stride. But the little boy hadn't called Chase "Daddy." Although he had allowed Chase to carry him to bed and/or to put him in and out of his car seat.

All in good time, she thought. Watching Chase with Eli, she knew this was where they belonged.

She'd spoken to her father twice since she'd come to stay with Chase on the ranch. Both times her father had begged forgiveness. Because she knew Jesus would expect her to do that, she had found it in her heart to forgive him. And so had Chase.

They'd even agreed to have her father visit them on the ranch over the upcoming weekend. It was a start. As much as she resented her father's interference with her life, she couldn't help but wonder if this hadn't been God's plan all along.

God had brought her and Chase together for Eli's sake. And that was a bond that would carry them forward. Or so she hoped.

Griff had let them know that Julia Stone was an alias for Tonya Redstone. Carl Longfoot had been a former boyfriend of Tonya's, and when Ian Dunlap had done the DNA tracing, it turned out Carl was Alecia's biological father. Carl had no knowledge of the kidnapping, and his alibi had proven he wasn't involved.

Tonya and her cousin Joshua had concocted the scheme with the help of their grandfather, Hank Redstone. And all three of them would go to jail for a very long time.

She smiled at Chase walking beside Eli. Chase had been spending as much time with Eli as possible, and it showed.

"Good job, Eli," Chase praised. "Are you ready to get down?"

"Yes," Eli said. When Chase lifted him off the horse, Eli wrapped his arms around Chase's neck. "Thanks, Daddy."

Wyn's eyes filled with tears as Chase hugged Eli close and kissed the top of his head. "I love you, buddy."

Eli paused, then said, "I love you and Mommy too."

Chase turned and crossed over to where she stood waiting. Rocky was there, too, as if to make sure nothing bad happened to Eli. Chase set Eli down next to Rocky, and the two ran up toward the cabin.

"Did you hear that?" Chase asked as he slid his arm around her waist.

"I did. I'm so happy for you, Chase." She kissed his cheek. "You're an awesome dad."

"I think that makes it official." Chase pulled a small ring box from his pocket. "I bought this for you a little over five years ago. Wynona, will you please marry me?"

"Yes, Chase. Yes, I'll marry you." She laughed when he swept her off her feet, twirled her around, and kissed her before setting her back down. "I would have said yes back then too."

"That's nice to know," Chase admitted. He took a moment to slide the modest engagement ring on her finger, then glanced over to where Eli was standing beside Rocky. "Yet despite missing out on Eli's early years, I somehow think this is the way things were meant to be. That this was exactly God's plan for us."

She hugged him close. "I agree."

"We'll have to let your father know we're getting married when he comes up to visit." Chase flashed a wicked grin. "I can't wait to tell him he's going to be stuck with me as a son-in-law after all."

"He'll be okay with that." Her father looked as if he'd aged ten years in the time she'd spent off the reservation.

And as much as she loved him, she wasn't going to live her life the way her father had planned. Her father had tried to force her to stay on the rez. His actions had caused the exact opposite of what he'd intended.

"Your father is welcome here to visit anytime." Chase's expression turned serious. "And I would never stop you and Eli from visiting him either."

"I know, and that's just one of the many reasons I love you." She gazed around the ranch. "I might visit him, but I'll never leave. I love it here, and so does Eli. We belong here with you."

"I love you, Wyn." Chase kissed her again, and she knew she had found her home here on the Sullivan K9 Search and Rescue Ranch with her son and the man she loved.

She couldn't wait to become a part of the Sullivan family for good.

I HOPE you enjoyed Chase and Wynona's story in *Scent of Panic*. The Sullivans and their K9s are always finding a way to get into trouble. Jessica and Logan are no exception. Are you interested in reading *Scent of Peril*? Click here!

DEAR READER

Thanks for reading *Scent of Panic*! I hope you enjoyed Chase and Wynona's story. I am having fun with this new Sullivan K9 Search and Rescue series. If you've been following my books for a while, you know how much I love dogs. These adorable and amazing K9s are the true heroes of these stories. And stubborn Rocky was a blast to write!

Don't forget, you can purchase ebooks or audiobooks directly from my website will receive a 15% discount by using the code **LauraScott15**.

I adore hearing from my readers! I can be found through my website at https://www.laurascottbooks.com, via Facebook at https://www.facebook.com/LauraScottBooks, Instagram at https://www.instagram.com/laurascottbooks/, and Twitter https://twitter.com/laurascottbooks. Please take a moment to subscribe to my YouTube channel at youtube.com/@LauraScottBooks-wr1xl?sub_confirmation=1.   Also take a moment to sign up for my monthly newsletter to learn about my new book releases! All subscribers receive a free novella not available for purchase on any platform.

Until next time,
Laura Scott
PS: Read on for a sneak peek of *Scent of Peril*.

SCENT OF PERIL

Chapter One

Jessica Sullivan frowned when she spied Logan Fletcher's plane making a wide arc above the ranch. Logan hadn't mentioned stopping by, so she wasn't sure what had brought him to their neck of the woods. Since losing their parents five-and-a-half years ago, she lived on the Sullivan K9 Search and Rescue Ranch with her eight siblings. They'd turned the family's dude ranch into a search and rescue operation.

Eyeing Logan's plane, she had to acknowledge her feelings toward Logan were—complicated. She'd had a crush on him in high school while he'd been dating her best friend, Ella. Then Ella died of a drug overdose. Losing her friend had killed her crush as she'd held Logan responsible.

But he'd claimed he wasn't involved. That he'd never done drugs and hadn't even known Ella had started using them. Ella's brother, Ethan, had also blamed Logan. Eight years later, she'd managed to forgive him to a point. But their once-close relationship had been lost forever.

With a sigh, she glanced down at her K9, Teddy, a black Belgian sheepdog that had been trained as a narcotics dog. She'd worked for the TSA prior to her parents' deaths. Since returning to the ranch, she'd begun cross-training Teddy on people scents to help their search and rescue operations. She might be biased, but Teddy was a quick learner. And eager to please, unlike Chase's K9, Rocky. Spring was in the air, but there was still plenty of snow on the ground. Logan would land his prop plane on the makeshift air landing strip they kept plowed year-round specifically for this purpose. When it came to search and rescue, they never knew what method of travel they'd need to use.

"Come, Teddy." She turned her back on her three-bedroom cabin to trudge across the ranch. As she approached the air strip, she watched Logan land the plane with grace and skill. She had flown with him several times, along with Teddy, making sure her K9 wore earphones to protect his ears, and had to admit she trusted Logan's piloting skills. She stood off to the side with her dog, waiting for Logan to jump down from behind the pilot's seat.

"Jess!" He jogged toward her. "I'm glad you're here."

"I live here," she said dryly. When he flushed, she waved a hand. "Sorry, I didn't mean to sound sarcastic. What's going on?"

"I was flying near the Bighorn Mountains earlier when I spotted what appears to be a piece of a tail fin from a plane." His green eyes locked on hers. "I immediately thought of you. I think we should head over to check it out."

A piece from her parents' plane? Her heart thumped in her chest. Five-and-a-half years ago, she and her siblings had scoured the mountainside searching for their parents and the plane without success. As it happened, her parents were flying with a friend who had not installed a black box, which would have helped them locate the wreckage. "Where exactly did you spot it?"

"Easier if I show you." At her look of impatience, Logan shrugged. "To be honest, it's several miles from the projected path of your parents' route, so it's not within the usual search zone. But I circled around twice to log the location before heading here."

That made her frown. "It could be from any plane."

"Maybe." He agreed. "I still think it's worth checking out."

"Okay. Let me grab Teddy's gear." She didn't want to leave her K9 behind. "I'll make a few sandwiches too."

"That sounds good. I'll wait here." Logan gestured to his plane. "I'll do a quick maintenance check."

Jess knew Logan took his charter flying business seriously. He was more than the pilot; he performed all the maintenance work on his three different planes himself. She appreciated the extra safety precautions.

Despite losing her parents to a small plane crash, she wasn't afraid of flying. Thankfully, Teddy didn't mind flying either.

Returning to her cabin, she threw extra dog food, water, and K9 protective gear into a duffel. She took a few minutes to slap a couple of thick ham sandwiches together and packed them along with some additional items in a smaller backpack for herself. She already wore all-terrain boots, but she swapped out her regular hat and gloves for woolen ones. The weather was mild now, but it was better to be prepared.

"Come, Teddy." As she turned to head back outside, she debated letting Maya or Chase know her plans. Then she decided against it. There would be plenty of time to fill them in if they were able to find and retrieve the plane debris.

If she and Logan couldn't find it, there was no sense in

getting her older siblings' hopes up. As a family, they'd come to grips with their loss. Their faith in God and in knowing their parents had everlasting life with Jesus helped. It was the not knowing what had happened or why their parents' plane had crashed that hurt the most.

A mystery that remained unsolved all these years later.

She quickened her pace with the backpack snug over her shoulders and the duffel thumping along her side. Teddy trotted next to her, his snout in the air. Even when he wasn't working, Teddy eagerly explored his surroundings with his nose.

Logan stepped back from the plane, then crossed over to take the duffel from her. "I'll store this in the back. Go ahead and jump in."

This was a routine they'd done often, but Teddy's ears pricked forward as he sniffed the passenger seat of the plane. Then he abruptly sat and let out a sharp bark.

What in the world? This was Teddy's alert for scenting drugs.

She took a step back, wondering if something else had caught the K9's attention. Logan was still storing the duffel in the back, so she held Teddy's gaze. "Search! Search for peppers!" Peppers was the word she used for drugs. She didn't like calling them candy, the way some narcotics handlers did. She personally hated peppers, so that was the term she'd used for drugs, which she also despised. It seemed the most appropriate for working with Teddy.

Teddy jumped to all fours and sniffed the area around the plane again. Then in almost the exact same spot, he sat and let out a sharp bark.

"What's up with Teddy?" Logan asked.

She whirled to face him. "You tell me. He's alerting on drugs. Drugs, Logan. Since when do you transport drugs?"

"What are you talking about?" Logan reared back as if she'd slapped him. "I have never transported drugs."

"Wrong answer." She gestured toward Teddy. "Teddy alerted on the scent of drugs."

Logan frowned, then rushed forward to look around the interior of his plane. She stayed back, not sure she was ready to go anywhere with him.

Then he turned his expression grim as he held up a black glove. "My last charter passenger must have left this behind."

She walked forward to see it for herself. "You're saying that guy may have been carrying drugs?"

Logan glanced at Teddy. "Your dog seems to think so. That's the reason I was up over the mountains in the first place. I dropped this guy off at a small landing area that wasn't too far away from the location I spotted the tail fin. It's not like I search people who pay for transportation. He didn't appear to be under the influence or anything."

"Where did he come from?"

"Cheyenne." Logan frowned. "I have his name written down, but he paid in cash."

Her eyes narrowed. "And you didn't find that suspicious?"

A flash of anger darkened his eyes. "No, I didn't. Those who can afford to charter a private plane often pay in cash. There's no crime in hiring a plane. Doug paid me in cash back in January when he needed help. This is my business, remember? Besides, as I said, he seemed okay. Had a bunch of hunting and fishing gear."

"Hunting in April?" She scoffed. "Not likely."

"Wild turkey hunting is legal in April," Logan said. "And fly-fishing opens in April. Look, it's not my job to quiz these guys on their plans. He paid for a plane ride, and I flew him to his destination. End of story."

"Except it's not the end of the story," she shot back. "Teddy alerted on drugs. That means your guy could be up to no good."

Logan sighed and rubbed the back of his neck. "I know that now. What do you want me to do? Call the local police?"

She thought about that for a moment. They could alert her brother-in-law, Doug Bridges, about their suspicions. Doug was a former DEA agent who now worked for the Wyoming State Department of Criminal Investigations. The other option was to alert the game warden for the area. His name was Eddie Marsh.

"Jess, we don't know this guy is a criminal," Logan said. "He could have a legit prescription for pain meds. Or maybe he was carrying a small stash of weed."

"You're right." She knew she was overreacting. Maybe because of the way Ella had overdosed all those years ago. She hated the idea of drugs being so accessible. But Ella had made the decision to take them. A choice that had proven fatal. Jess shook off the depression. "Okay, fine. Let's go. But I hope you don't hear from that guy again. He may have a legit prescription, or he may not. This could be some new way of transporting drugs from one area of the state to the next."

Logan hesitated, then nodded. "I agree. I'll be too busy to take him on another trip."

A flash of guilt hit hard. This was Logan's livelihood. She had no right to ask him to turn down paying clients. Especially not during the colder months of the year when there were fewer tourists flocking to the area.

Still, turkey hunting and fly-fishing in April seemed a

stretch. Spring might be in the air, warming the daytime temperatures to a balmy forty to fifty degrees, but during the night, the temps dropped like a rock.

"Are you ready?" Logan sounded impatient.

"Yes. Get in, Teddy." She waved to the plane. She decided against rewarding her K9 for his alert since there was no way to prove the dog had actually scented drugs. After the dog gracefully jumped into the plane, she followed suit.

But as Logan went through his checklist for takeoff, she made a note to let Doug know about Teddy's alert when they returned. Better to play it safe.

Especially if the guy was up to no good.

LOGAN STARTED THE PLANE ENGINE, glancing at Teddy who wore earmuffs like a pro. He'd seen the Sullivan K9s in action on many occasions, but this was the first time he'd been on the receiving end of an alert.

Had Craig Benton, his last charter client, been transporting drugs? At the time, the guy hadn't seemed like someone who would be involved in that sort of thing. But now he kept seeing the roll of cash the guy had pulled from his pocket. Benton had peeled ten crisp one-hundred-dollar bills from the roll, handing them over without hesitation.

A drug dealer? Or just a rich guy looking to spend time in the mountains?

He turned his attention to flying the plane. He radioed the closest tower, located at the Yellowstone airport, to confirm his flight plan.

"Roger, two-five-seven, you're good to go," the dispatcher said.

"Ten-four," he responded. Sensing Jessica's gaze, he glanced over. "What?"

"Nothing. It's just that every time we fly, I think of my parents heading home from Billings." She waved a hand toward the Bighorn Mountains looming ahead. "I still don't understand why they crashed."

He thought about the jagged section of a tail fin he'd glimpsed from the sky. If he hadn't taken Craig Benton to meet his alleged hunting buddies at the base of the mountain, he wouldn't have seen it. "I'm sure it's not easy to move forward without answers."

She nodded without saying anything. He might have wished things could be different between him and Jess, but Ella's death loomed large between them. For the hundredth time, he wished he'd never asked Ella out. That he'd never gotten involved with the prettiest girl in their high school class in the first place.

But he had. And his life had been forever changed by her death.

Jess hadn't been the only one who'd stared at him with accusing eyes. Ella's brother, Ethan, had been extremely vocal. The local sheriff's department had executed a search warrant on his house, his car, and his plane. They hadn't found any drugs, but most of the townsfolk had assumed he'd gotten rid of the evidence.

Eventually the whispers had stopped. But he knew there were still people in Cody who blamed him for Ella's death.

Like Jess. Oh, she'd claimed that was nothing more than ancient history, but the old feelings had resurfaced after Teddy had alerted on the scent of drugs in his plane. The way she'd glared at him with suspicion had struck deep in his core.

He banked the Cessna to the right. Jessica leaned

forward, searching the ground below. "We're still ten minutes from the general area," he told her.

She nodded to indicate she'd heard but continued scanning the rocky terrain below. No doubt, she was hoping to spot additional debris.

He understood her desire for answers. He'd logged countless flight hours while searching for her parents' plane. Chase had insisted on paying for his fuel and time, and he'd only accepted because he'd been forced to turn away paying jobs in order to continue making flights to the mountainside and back. Something he wouldn't have been able to do without the additional financial help.

The entire Sullivan family had been very grateful for his efforts. Even Jess.

He'd have given anything to have found something useful back then. And he had never stopped searching during his flights.

He hoped this bit of plane debris would bring some answers.

Using the landmark of a jagged rock poking out from the side of the mountain, he slowly dropped the plane's altitude. Tracking the rocky outcropping, he turned twenty degrees, then peered down through his side window.

"There it is!" He couldn't hide his excitement. "Do you see it?"

"I think so." Jess's voice was uncertain. "I mean, I see something white, but I can't tell what it is from here."

"Hang on, I'll circle around so we can get a little lower." He banked the plane in an arc, putting some distance between the plane and the trees leering upward from the mountain.

He took the Cessna down another few hundred feet. This was the best he could do without risking the tops of some of the tree branches scraping along the underbelly of the plane.

"I think you're right," Jess said. "I can tell that it looks like the tail of a plane."

"I'll see if I can find a place to land." He knew without being told that Jess wanted to retrieve the piece of debris. "But it will be a long hike."

"I know, but we have plenty of daylight left." She glanced at him. "It's only noon. We'll eat our lunch and head out. We should be able to get there and back to the plane in plenty of time."

"Okay." He knew the mountains could be deceptive when it came to distance. What looked like an hour-long hike was likely triple that time frame. Especially since there was still plenty of snow covering the ground.

But this was why he'd brought her to the area, so there was no point in complaining. Thankfully, he always carried plenty of winter-weather gear. He wasn't nearly as worried about the elements as he was about potentially damaging his plane. He scanned the area below. "Help me spot an area to land."

Jess was silent for a moment. He noticed the long, flat stretch of land at the same time she did. "How about there?"

"It could be private property." It seemed as if the stretch of land had been used as a landing strip in the past as it was cleared of snow and brush. It wasn't the one he'd used to drop off Craig Benton, but it wasn't that far away either. He didn't see a sign of a dwelling nearby. After a moment's hesitation, he shrugged. "Okay, that will work. Hang on."

Jess nodded. She wasn't a nervous flier, taking the usual air pocket bumps in stride. He turned again so he could approach the strip of open land straight on, then brought the plane in for a landing.

The minute he brought the Cessna to a stop, Jess ripped her headphones off and turned to remove the headgear from her dog. He shouldn't have been surprised at how Teddy seemed to enjoy flying as much as Jess did.

"Down, Teddy." Jess jumped down from the plane. Her dog followed suit. Then she snagged her backpack and pulled out two thick sandwiches. "Here you go."

"Thanks." He gratefully took the sandwich. "We'll need to make sure we gear up," he said between bites. The weather in spring could be dicey. There were no storms in the forecast earlier, but that could easily change without warning. "We need to be prepared for anything."

"I know. That's why I brought my backpack and Teddy's duffel." She ate her sandwich, too, while rummaging in the duffel for her dog's equipment. The Sullivans always cared for their dogs before themselves.

After Jess finished eating, she placed a vest over Teddy's torso and added padded booties over his paws. Logan checked his own pack, taking note of the bottles of water, protein bars, and dried fruit and nut packs that would have to serve as a late snack or early dinner if needed. When Jess had finished with Teddy, who surprisingly didn't seem to mind the booties, he handed her half his rations. "We may need these later."

"Thank you." Her smile made his pulse jump. He forced himself to ignore the response. He was the last person Jess would consider dating, and the sooner he came to grips with that fact, the better.

"Anytime." They took a moment to tuck the supplies away before donning their thick outer gear. Jess stuffed some dog food into her backpack. They each had a pack, so he couldn't carry hers. "I have room if you need more supplies."

"This should be fine." She bent to give her dog some water from a collapsible dish. Then she straightened and tucked the dish into the pack. "Okay, we're ready."

"Let's do this." He headed off across the open stretch of land toward the woods surrounding the base of the mountain. Double-checking his compass, he verified they were headed in the correct direction.

Teddy navigated the rugged terrain without difficulty. He and Jess took things more slowly. It wasn't just the snow-covered rocks and fallen branches, but there was no distinct path for them to follow. They had to forge their own way, often through thick brush.

They didn't talk much, conserving their strength for the hike. After about forty minutes, Jess lifted her hand. "I'd like to give Teddy a break."

"I need it more than he does," he joked, sitting on a fallen log. Jess dropped beside him.

"Me too. I haven't given Teddy the search command to track anything, but the way he's sniffing around, I'm sure he's burning as much energy as if he were on the hunt."

Teddy sat beside her, looking up at her adoringly. The dog was protective of her, but thankfully, he didn't view Logan as a threat.

He double-checked his compass. Years of flying had honed his sense of direction, and he could easily picture the area where they'd spied the plane piece in his mind. "We're on the right trajectory. But we still have a good three miles to go."

"Okay." She took a sip of water, then passed the bottle to him. "That shouldn't be a problem."

He didn't doubt her ability to keep up. Over the five years that the Sullivan family had been working search and rescue, he'd noticed they'd gotten in prime physical shape.

He'd been so shallow in high school, far too concerned with dating the pretty, popular girl, that he'd overlooked the sweet and kind Jessica.

Reminding himself there was no point in reliving the past, he tucked the water bottle into his backpack, then stood and stretched. "Ready?"

"Yes." She rose to her feet. "Come, Teddy."

As if the dog wouldn't follow, he thought with a wry smile. With his black coat and protective nature, Teddy's name should have been Shadow.

They hiked for another thirty minutes, mostly in silence. Their conversation consisted of warning each other about environmental hazards such as fallen logs or the sudden appearance of a creek. Teddy forged ahead, then turned to wait for them to catch up before bounding forward again.

"He acts as if he knows our final destination," Logan said.

"I've noticed that too." She tracked the dog with her gaze. "Maybe he's just glad to be out in the wilderness."

He nodded. Jess would know her dog better than he did.

They stopped for another break. He checked his compass. "We're making good time," he said. "I estimate we have another thirty to forty minutes to go."

She gave her dog some water, then tipped her head back to gaze up at the sky. "As much as I hate daylight savings time, it's nice to know we have several hours of sunlight left."

He grunted in agreement.

After a ten-minute rest, they continued moving through the brush. He broke through a particularly dense section of woods to find the clearing.

"I don't remember seeing this from the plane," Jess said with a frown. "Do you?"

"Not really." He pulled out his compass again to verify their location. "We may have veered slightly off course to the south. We'll need to turn north, up the slope."

"Okay." She flashed a grin. "At least heading back to the plane should be easier."

He took the lead, noticing that Teddy stayed closer to Jessica's side now. He didn't see any people tracks in the snow, so he didn't anticipate danger from a human perspective.

Wild animals were another story.

He made another correction in their path, then continued climbing. When he crested a hill, he stopped and swung his gaze to the right.

"I see it!" Quickening his pace, he slipped and slid on the snow toward the metal object that was larger here than he'd anticipated. He bent and picked up the large chunk of metal that was clearly from a small plane.

"Are there any markings on it?" Jess was breathless as she joined him. Teddy, too, sniffed at the metal with interest.

He carefully turned the tail fin in his hands. "No, I don't see any markings. Other than the rust from being in the elements."

Jess frowned. "So we really can't say for sure that this is a part of my parents' plane."

"No, we can't. But we can have it tested. Maybe there's a forensic way to identify how long this has been lying here."

"I like that idea." Jess's blue eyes filled with hope. "I'm so glad we came."

He was too. Anything for her to look at him like that.

A crack of gunfire rang out. Dropping the tail fin, Logan grabbed Jess's arm, pulling her toward the closest tree. But she jerked free to turn toward her dog. "Teddy, come!"

The dog ran toward her as another shot rang out,

striking the tree not far from Jess. She threw herself over Teddy, hauling the dog behind the tree. Logan covered Jess's body with his, his mind racing. That last bullet had been too close for comfort. Whoever was shooting at them wasn't hunting for wild turkeys.

Was this about his recent charter? Or something else?

Logan could only hope they'd survive long enough to find out.

Made in United States
Cleveland, OH
09 August 2025

19272062R00138